W9-BGO-281

Dear Reader,

We are deeply saddened to have to say goodbye to Betty Neels, who was one of our best-loved authors, as well as being a wonderfully warm and thoroughly charming woman. She led a fascinating life even before becoming a writer, and her publishing record was impressive.

Over her thirty-year career, Betty wrote more than 134 novels, and published in more than one hundred international markets. She continued to write into her ninetieth year, remaining as passionate about her characters and stories then as she was in her very first book. Betty Neels was prolific, and we have a number of new titles to feature in our forthcoming publishing programs.

Betty will be greatly missed, both by her friends within Harlequin and by her legions of loyal readers around the world. Our deepest sympathy and condolences are with her family at this time.

Yours sincerely,

Harlequin Books

Betty Neels spent her childhood and youth in Devonshire before training as a nurse and midwife. She was an army nursing sister during the war, married a Dutchman and subsequently lived in Holland for fourteen years. Betty started to write on retirement from nursing, incited by a lady in a library bemoaning the lack of romance novels. She has become a prolific and well-loved author.

THE BEST *of*

BETTY NEELS

THE FIFTH DAY
OF CHRISTMAS

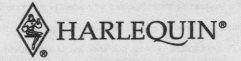

HARLEQUIN®

TORONTO • NEW YORK • LONDON
AMSTERDAM • PARIS • SYDNEY • HAMBURG
STOCKHOLM • ATHENS • TOKYO • MILAN • MADRID
PRAGUE • WARSAW • BUDAPEST • AUCKLAND

ISBN 0-373-51163-9

THE FIFTH DAY OF CHRISTMAS

First North American Publication 2001

CHAPTER ONE

VIEWED FROM the comparative comfort of the ambulance's interior, the M1 looked uninviting. Miss Julia Pennyfeather, too occupied with her patient to have bothered overmuch with the passing scenery, now realised that the motorway was becoming more and more shrouded in fog, which, coupled with the fast darkening sky of a December afternoon, boded ill for their chances of reaching their destination as early as they had hoped. She pulled her cloak closely around her, cast a quick look at her dozing patient and peered out once more. There seemed to be a lot of traffic surging past, at great speed and in a confusion of lights, a sight which made her thankful that she wasn't called upon to drive the ambulance. She frowned in thought, then, moving cautiously, opened the little glass window behind the driving seat and said softly to the man sitting beside the driver, 'Willy—the fog, it's getting worse, isn't it?'

The man the back of whose neck she had addressed turned a cheerful face to answer her. 'Proper thick, Nurse, but it's not all that far. We're coming up to Newcastle now; it's about sixty miles to the Border and another twelve to the crossroads where we turn off—and the house is another ten miles or so.'

'It's nearly four o'clock,' said Julia. 'We shan't get there much before nine...'

'Just in nice time for a bit o' supper, Nurse, before we 'ands over the patient and goes to our warm beds.'

They were off the motorway now and almost clear of Newcastle; two hours' steady driving would bring them to the Border, and once they were in Scotland... She broke off her speculations as the girl on the stretcher asked, 'Where are we, Nurse?'

Julia told her, adding in a determinedly cheerful voice, 'We shan't be long now—three hours at the most, perhaps less. I expect you'd like a drink, wouldn't you?' She unscrewed a vacuum flask and poured the milkless tea into a mug. 'As soon as we arrive, you shall have your insulin and your supper—I'm sure they'll have it ready for you, for your nurse will have arrived some time this afternoon.'

'I hope I like her.'

Julia glanced at her patient. 'I'm sure you will,' she replied in a soothing voice, and privately hoped that she was right. Miss Mary MacGall hadn't been the easiest of patients—eighteen years old, pretty and spoilt and a diabetic who somehow never managed to achieve stabilisation, she had been a handful the Private Wing of St Clare's Hospital had been glad to see go. In the two short weeks she had been there, having an acute appendix removed, and then, unfortunately, peritonitis, which naturally played havoc with the diabetes, she had been rude to the Matron, flirted outrageously with the young housemen, and exasperated the consultant staff; only with Julia was she amenable, and that was something neither Julia nor her fellow workers could fathom, unless it was that Julia's dark and striking beauty was such a magnificent foil to her own blonde prettiness. And Julia didn't fuss, but treated her with the pleasant calm that a well-trained nanny might have shown to a recalcitrant child. Not that Julia looked in the least like a nanny—indeed, just the opposite, with her almost black hair and great brown eyes with their preposterously long lashes. Her mouth was a little large perhaps, but beautifully shaped and her nose was straight, with the merest hint of a tilt at its tip. She was well above average height, nicely rounded and refreshingly and completely nat ural. She was just twenty-two and had achieved State Registration only a few months previously. And only the day before she had left the hospital where she had spent several happy, busy years, not because she had particularly wanted to, but to look after her sister-in-law who had just had a second child and was suffering from depression. It had been, therefore, a happy chance that Mary MacGall should have demanded to be sent home by ambulance, and also demanded, at the same time, that Julia should go with her on the journey. Julia was due to leave anyway, and it would give her a couple of days' respite before she went home.

When next Julia looked out of the window it was snowing hard and the fog had become dense. The ambulance was travelling slowly now, with its blue light flashing, and Julia was uneasily aware that they were skidding from time to time. She opened the little window once more and said softly into Willy's ear, 'Is it freezing as well?'

He nodded without looking round.

'Are we lost?'

She heard his chuckle and took comfort from the

sound. 'Not a bit of it, Nurse. We're over the Border—we'll be at the crossroads soon.'

'Is Bert all right? Does he want to stop?'

She peered ahead, the visibility was down to about ten yards and that was obscured by driving snow.

Bert answered for himself. 'I'm OK, Nurse. It's not far now and I think we'd do better to keep going. It might clear.'

She agreed softly, knowing that he had said that to reassure her, and closed the window, observing for the benefit of her patient,

'We've a dozen miles or so to go. Are you very hungry? I've some cream crackers here and there's plenty of tea.'

But Mary was disposed to be difficult. She said rather peevishly,

'I want a huge steak with lots of duchesse potatoes and creamed cauliflower and lashings of gravy and sauce, then Charlotte Russe with masses of whipped cream and a plate of petits fours—the gooey ones, and a huge whisky and soda—oh, and Kummel with my coffee.'

Julia felt sympathy with her patient. After all, she was very young; she would be on a fixed diet for the rest of her life. It was a pity that she was so spoiled that she refused to accept the fact, and anyway, once she was stabilised, the diet wouldn't be too awful, for her parents were wealthy enough to give it the variety those in more straitened circumstances couldn't afford. She said kindly, 'You make me feel quite hungry too, but you'd pay for it afterwards, you know.'

The girl beside her scowled. 'Who cares? That's what you're for—to see that I don't die in a coma.'

Julia looked at her reflectively. 'There's always the possibility that someone might not be there...'

'Oh, yes, there will,' declared Mary, and sat up suddenly. 'I suppose you wouldn't like to stay with me—for ever, I mean.'

Julia smiled, feeling a little touched. 'How nice of you to ask me. But I have to go home and look after my sister-in-law for a bit, then I thought I'd get a job abroad for a year or two—and I've still got my midwifery to do.'

'Marry a rich man instead.'

'Why rich? As long as he's the right one, the money doesn't matter very much, does it? You need enough to live on and educate the children.'

'And pretty clothes and the hairdresser and jewellery and going to the theatre and out to dine, and a decent holiday at least twice a year.'

Julia said soberly, 'Perhaps I'm not ambitious,' and turned away to look out of the window again—a pointless act, for it had been quite dark for some time now.

When the ambulance at last stopped, Julia couldn't believe they had arrived, for the last hour had been a nightmare of skidding and crawling through the blanket of fog and snow and now there was a gale blowing as well. She stepped out of the ambulance into several inches of snow and then clutched at her cap as a gust of wind tossed her backwards as though she had been a leaf. It was pitch dark too, but in the ambulance lights she could just see the beginning of steps leading upwards. She stood aside to let Bert and Willy get into the ambulance and asked, 'Shall I ring the bell?' and thought how ridiculous it sounded in this black waste of snow and fog and howling wind. But Bert said cheerfully enough,

'OK, Nurse—up them steps, and look out for the ice.'

She advanced cautiously with the beam of her powerful torch guiding her: it wasn't so bad after all—the steps ended at a great door upon whose knocker she beat a brisk tattoo, and when she saw the brass bell in the wall, she rang that for good measure. But there were no lights—she peered around her, unable to see anything but the reassuring solidarity of the door before her, and that hadn't opened. She was about to go down the steps again to relay her doubts to her companions when the door swung open, revealing a very old man holding a hurricane lantern. She was still getting her breath when he spoke testily.

'Ye didna' need to make all that noise. I heard ye the fust time.'

Julia, who had nice manners, apologised. 'Is this Drumlochie House?' she asked through teeth which were beginning to chatter with the cold.

'Aye—ye'll be the nurse with Miss Mary?'

'That's right—could you turn on the lights, please, so that the ambulance men can bring her indoors?'

'No lights,' said the old man without annoyance. 'Wind's taken the electric—can't think how ye got here.'

Julia couldn't either, but it hardly seemed the right moment to discuss it. She said instead, 'Then would you leave the door open and we'll bring Miss Mary in.'

She didn't wait to hear his reply but went carefully down the steps again.

She followed the two men, with the carrying chair and Mary in it, between them, back up again, shuddering at the possibility of a broken ankle or two added to Mary's diabetes. But they achieved the entrance without mishap and went inside where the old man was waiting for them, his lamp held high. 'So ye're back, Miss Mary,' he was, it seemed, a man of few words, 'your room's ready.'

He turned and started to walk across the hall towards the staircase discernible in the gloom, and the ambulance men, still with Mary between them, followed him with Julia bringing up the rear, shivering a little partly because she had got cold waiting at the front door and partly because her surroundings were, inadequately lighted as they were, a trifle forbidding. They seemed to walk a great distance before the old man at length opened a door and they entered Mary's bedroom—a large apartment with a fire burning in its open fireplace and most pleasantly furnished. Julia, looking round her, heaved a sigh of relief. If their rooms were half as comfortable they would have nothing to grumble about.

'Where's the nurse?' she asked the old man.

He stood and thought, his head on one side, for an aggravating moment. 'The nurse? Weel, she's to come from Edinburgh, but it's been snowing a blizzard since daybreak hereabouts. There'll be no nurse.'

'No nurse!' Julia looked at him with something like horror. 'But I'm going back to London with the ambulance in the morning—I can't leave my patient. Where's the telephone?'

'The wind's had it.'

The wind, thought Julia bitterly, was answerable for a lot.

'There must be some way of getting a message—to the village or a doctor—or the police.'

He didn't even bother to say no, just shook his head. 'Snow's deep,' he observed without emotion. 'There's Jane the cook and Madge the maid gone to Hawick yesterday to shop for Miss Mary's return. They'll not be back for twa days, maybe.'

Julia's dismay was smothered in a flood of practical thoughts.

'Food?' she asked. 'Hot water, candles?'

'Food's enough—candles and lamps we've got—hot water, now, that's another matter. I've no call for hot water, stove's gone out.'

'If you could possibly light it for us again? Miss Mary—all of us, we need to wash at least. Are there any rooms ready for us?'

He shook his head. 'No. Madge was to have done that, and me thinking ye'd not get here in this weather—I didna' light the fire…'

'Never mind—could the ambulance men come and help you? They're tired and hungry—they must have a meal and a good sleep. If you'd give them the bed-linen I'm sure they'll make up the beds, and I'll come down to the kitchen and cook something.'

He looked at her with a glimmer of respect. 'Aye, do that if ye will. Miss Mary—she's all right?'

'Once she has had her supper she will be.' Julia smiled at him and went to fetch Bert and Willy.

There was food enough once she could find it in the vast semi-basement kitchen. She pottered about, still wrapped in her cloak, while the men made up beds and lighted fires, making Mary's supper as attractive as possible.

It was getting on for midnight when Julia removed the supper tray, and Mary, still grumbling, had consented to go to bed. Julia left an oil lamp the old man had produced in the room, wished her patient a good night and went in search of Willy and Bert. She found them, after a great deal of tramping up and down draughty corridors, very snug in a little room on the floor above.

'Nothing but fourposters downstairs,' Willy explained. 'We've found you a nice room below, Nurse, got a fire going an' all. First left at the bottom of the stairs.'

She thanked them, warned them that she was about to cook supper and went in search of her sleeping quarters. The room was reasonably near her patient's, she was glad to find, and at the head of the stairs, and although there was a piercing draught whistling round the hall below, the room itself looked pleasant enough. She sighed with relief, went to look at Mary, who was already asleep, and made her way downstairs once more. The old man had disappeared; to bed probably, having considered that he had done enough for them. She set about frying eggs and bacon and boiling the kettle for tea, and presently the three of them sat down to a supper, which, while not being quite what they had expected, was ample and hot.

The three of them washed up, wished each other good night, and crept upstairs, bearing a variety of candlesticks and yawning their heads off. Julia, with a longing eye on the comfort of the bed, undressed with the speed of lightning, unpinned her hair, brushed it perfunctorily and went to find a bathroom. There were several, none supplying more than tepid water, so she cleaned her teeth, washed her face and hands with the same speed with which she had brushed her hair and, after a quick look at the sleeping Mary, retired to her room, where, without daring to take off her dressing gown, she jumped into bed. And as she closed her eyes the front door bell rang.

She waited a moment, pretending to herself that she hadn't heard it, but when it pealed again she got out of bed, picked up her torch, thrust her feet into slippers and started downstairs. The wind was fiercer now and the draughts eddied around her, chilling her to the bone. Only the thought of the unfortunate person on the doorstep urged her on. It would be the nurse, arrived by some miracle Julia was far too tired to investigate, or perhaps the cook and the maid from Hawick, although she fancied that the town was a good many miles away. She undid the bolts of the front door, slid the chain back and opened its creaking weight on to the fog and wind and snow outside.

There was a man on the top step, a very large man, who stood wordless and patient while she allowed her torch to travel his considerable length. She knew that he was staring at her from the gloom and when she said impatiently, 'Oh, do come in—we'll both catch our deaths of cold...' he stepped into the hall without uttering a word, only when he had locked the door behind her did he say without heat,

'Of all the damn fool things to do—opening a door to a complete stranger in the dead of night!'

Julia's beautiful eyes opened wide. 'But you rang the bell.'

'And have you never heard of opening a door on its chain? I might have been armed with a shotgun.'

Julia interrupted him in a matter-of-fact voice, 'Don't be absurd—who'd be out on a night like this with a shotgun?'

He laughed then. 'Since you're kind enough to trust me, could I beg shelter until the morning? I'm on my way down from Edinburgh and quite obviously I've taken the wrong road.'

He gave himself a shake and the snow tumbled off him, to lie unmelting on the floor. 'You're not alone in this place?'

'No,' said Julia with calm, 'I'm not—there are two ambulance men asleep upstairs, so tired they won't hear a sound—and my patient—oh, and there's a kind of ancient family retainer, but I haven't seen him for several hours.'

He took the torch from her hand and shone it deliberately on her.

'You are a fool,' he remarked mildly. 'Here you are, a very beautiful girl unless my eyes deceive me, with two men sleeping like the dead upstairs, an old retainer who's probably deaf and a patient chained to his bed...'

'Look,' said Julia patiently, 'I'm very tired—you're welcome to a bed,' she waved a vague arm towards the staircase. 'There are plenty of empty rooms if you like to choose one. Are you hungry?'

She had taken the torch once more from his grasp and shone it briefly on him. 'Take off that coat,' she advised. 'I'll go and put the kettle on—will bacon and eggs do?'

'Not only beautiful but kind too,' he murmured.

'Thank you, I'm famished. Where's the kitchen? Go back to bed and I'll look after myself.'

She was already on her way kitchenwards. 'It's warmer there than anywhere else. Come along.'

Ten minutes later he was sitting at the kitchen table devouring the food she had cooked, while she made the tea. 'Thank heaven there's a gas stove,' Julia commented as she fetched two cups. 'The wind took the electric and the telephone.'

'How very whimsical!'

Julia poured him another cup of tea and then filled her own cup. In the little silence which followed a clock wheezed dryly and struck twice, and the wind, taking on a new strength, howled like a banshee round the house. Julia looked up to see the stranger's eyes fastened on her. He smiled and said, 'If you trust me, go to bed—I'll clear up and find myself a room.'

She got to her feet and picked up her torch, yawning as she did so. 'There's your candle,' she indicted a brass candlestick with its snuffer which she had put ready for him. 'Don't come into my room, will you? It's at the top of the stairs—nor the third one on the right—that's my patient's. Good night.'

She wondered why he looked amused as he wished her good night, getting politely to his feet as he did so, which small action somehow reassured her.

Not that she needed reassuring, she told herself, lying curled up in her chilly bed; the fire had died down and the warmth it had engendered had already been swallowed up by the icy air. She shivered and decided that she liked him, even though she knew nothing about him, neither his name nor his business, but she liked his face—a face she felt she could trust, with strong features and steady blue eyes and a mouth that was firm and kind. And even though he had called her a fool—which she was bound to admit was the truth—he had also called her beautiful. She fell uneasily asleep, smiling a little.

Something wakened her in the pitch darkness, a sound, not repeated. She switched on the torch to find that it was just after six o'clock, and sat up in bed, the better to listen. The sound came again—a hoarse croak. She was out of bed, thrusting her feet into her slippers as the list of post-operative complications liable to follow an appendicectomy on a diabetic patient unfolded itself in her still tired mind. Carbuncles, gangrene, broncho-pneumonia…the croak came again which effectively ruled out the first two, and when she reached her patient's bedroom and saw Mary's flushed face as she lay shivering in bed, she was almost sure that it was the third.

As she approached the bed Mary said irritably, 'I feel so ill, and I can't stop coughing—it hurts.'

'I'll sit you up a bit,' said Julia with a calm she didn't feel. Sudden illness on a hospital ward was one thing, but in an isolated house cut off from the outside world, it was quite a different matter. She fetched more pillows and propped the girl up, took her temperature which was as high as she had expected it to be, and gave her a drink, while all the time she was deciding what to do. Presently, when Mary was as comfortable as she could be made, Julia said,

'I'm going to send someone for the doctor—once we've got you on an antibiotic you'll feel better within hours. Will you stay quietly until I come back?'

She found the stranger in the third room she looked into, lying on his back on a vast fourposter bed, fast asleep. She put out an urgent hand and tapped a massive shoulder and he opened his eyes at once, staring at her with a calm which she found most comforting.

Before she could speak he said reflectively, 'The hair's a little wild, but I still think you're a beautiful girl. What's the matter?'

Julia swept her long black hair impatiently on one side the better to see him. 'My patient—she's ill. I'm afraid I must ask you to go and find a doctor or a telephone or—or something. I can't ask the ambulance men to go; they've got to go back to London today and they must have a night's sleep.'

He had sat up and swung his legs over the side of the bed. 'And I, being a man of leisure, am the obvious one to sacrifice on the altar of frostbite and exposure.'

Julia just stopped herself in time from wringing her hands. 'I'd go myself, but who's to look after Mary if I do?'

'A moot point,' he conceded, and stood up, reassuringly large. 'And before I detect the first rising note of hysteria in your very delightful voice, I must tell you that I am a doctor.'

Julia's first reaction was one of rage. 'You beast,' she said roundly, 'letting me get all worried!'

He smiled at her and lifted her neatly to sit on the bed and then sat down beside her. 'I am of the opinion that if I were not a doctor I should even now be meekly dressing myself, preparatory to tramping miles in search of aid, while you coped with great competence with whatever crisis has arisen. Now, let's have the bad news.'

She shivered, and was glad when he put an arm around her shoulders.

'My patient's a diabetic—an unstabilised one. She had appendicectomy followed by peritonitis two weeks ago. She made a good recovery although she isn't very co-operative and has had several slight co- mas. She wanted—insisted on coming home and it was arranged that she should travel from St Clare's in London by ambulance. We had a job getting here, but on the whole she had a comfortable journey and her usual diet and insulin. Her TPR was normal last night. She's loaded with sugar and acetone now and her temp's a hundred and three.'

He got off the bed, taking her with him. 'Well, you pop back to the patient and make soothing sounds while I put on some clothes and fetch my case—it's locked in the car just outside the door.' He gave her a gentle push. 'Go along now, there's a good girl.'

Mary was restless when Julia got back to her. She said as soon as she caught sight of her, 'I'm going to die, and there isn't a doctor.'

Julia gave her another drink of water and then went to build up the fire. 'Yes, there is.' She explained about his arrival during the night in a few bi* *i* words because Mary was too feverish to concentrate on any- thing. 'He'll be here in a moment,' went on Julia soothingly, 'he'll take a look at you and then pre- scribe something which will have you feeling better in no time.'

She went and got the case history notes and the charts and diets she had prepared so carefully for the

nurse who was to have taken over from her, laid them
neatly on a table and then hastily plaited her hair. She
had just finished doing that when the doctor knocked
on the door and came in.

Not only had he donned his clothes, but a faultless
professional manner with them, which somehow
made the whole situation seem normal and not in the
least worrying. He knew what he was about, for he
dealt with his patient gently and with a calm air of
assurance which convinced her that she was already
getting better, and then went to bend over Julia's pa-
pers, lying ready for them. When he had finished
reading them he looked up and asked,

'Is there a doctor's letter?'

'Yes,' said Julia, 'it's in my room.' She didn't offer
to fetch it.

'I think I should see it—I'll take full responsibility
for opening it, Nurse. Would you fetch it?'

She did so without a word, not sure as to the ethics
of the case, and stood quietly by while he read it.
Which he did, refolding it into its envelope when he
had finished and adding some writing of his own before handing it back to her.

'Penicillin, I think, Nurse. Shall we give her a shot
now and repeat it six-hourly? And the insulin—she's
been on Semilente, I see. We'd better increase it this
morning and test every two hours until this evening.
Now, diet…'

He went away when he had given Mary her penicillin and told her cheerfully that she would be out of
bed in a couple of days, leaving Julia to reiterate all
he had said before she went to dress. Once more in
uniform and intent on perching her cap on her neatly

arranged hair, she turned in surprise when there was a tap on her door.

'Tea,' said the stranger, 'and if you'll tell me where the ambulance men are I'll wake them for you.'

Julia took the proffered cup. 'How kind,' she said with surprise, and felt suddenly downcast when he answered carelessly,

'Oh, I'm handy about the house,' for it made him sound as though he were married. She said hastily because she wanted to change the trend of her thoughts, 'Is the weather better?'

He sat down on the end of the bed and started to drink the ambulance men's tea. 'No—the snow's in drifts—the car's almost covered and so is the ambulance. There's no snow at present, but there's more to come as far as I can see in this light. The fog has lifted, but the ground's like glass.'

She sipped her tea. It looked as though they would be there for another day at least and she was surprised to find that she didn't mind in the least. When he asked, 'What's your name?' she answered without hesitation. 'Pennyfeather, Julia Pennyfeather.'

'Miss Pennyfeather—it is Miss?'

She nodded. 'You're drinking Willy's and Bert's teas,' she pointed out.

'I'm thirsty. Don't you want to know my name?'

She nodded again.

'Van den Werff—Ivo. Very nearly thirty years old and until now, a confirmed bachelor.'

She ignored her sudden delight. 'Dutch?' she hazarded. 'Do you work in England—no, Scotland?'

'I've been on a course at the Royal Infirmary in

Edinburgh. I'm on my way back to Holland, but I intend to spend a day or so in London before I cross.'

Julia drank her tea, conscious of a sense of loss because presently he would be gone and she would never see him again. He got up off the bed and picked up the tray with the two empty cups and went off.

Julia went downstairs herself a few minutes later and found the old man sitting by the gas stove, drinking tea. She said good morning pleasantly and was told there was nothing good about it, so she busied herself getting her patient's diet and went back upstairs with it. It was another ten minutes by the time she had given the insulin and arranged Mary more comfortably to have her tea and bread and butter, and when she got back to the kitchen the old man had gone. She set about laying the table and got out the frying pan once more; lucky that there were plenty of eggs and a quantity of bacon, she thought, peering into the old-fashioned, roomy larder. She was making the tea when the three men came in, Willy and Bert very apologetic at having slept through the night's calamities. They looked well rested though, and volunteered cheerfully to do any chores she might choose to set them.

Bert looked at Julia an asked worriedly, 'And what's to be done about you, Nurse? We'll 'ave to go the minute we can—will you be able to come with us? You can't stay here alone.'

'She won't be alone.' The doctor's quiet voice sounded quite certain about that. 'I'll stay until the patient's own doctor can take over and the nurse can get here.'

'That's quite unnecessary,' said Julia quickly, 'I'm

perfectly able to manage...' she remembered how she had awakened him that morning and went faintly pink, and before she could finish what she was going to say, Bert observed with obvious relief, 'Ah, well, if the doc's going to be 'ere, that's OK, ain't it, Willy? Can't do better than that.'

'Then that's settled,' said Dr van den Werff, ignoring the light of battle in Julia's fine eyes. 'In any case, we can do nothing today except get this mausoleum warm. If the snow holds off we might reconnoitre later on...in the meantime shall we share out the chores?'

Something which he did with a pleasant authority which neither Willy nor Bert disputed, and which Julia, even if she had wished to do so, was unable to argue against because she had to go back to her patient, leaving him to explain to the old reta r, who had appeared from nowhere to join them at breakfast, just why they were forced to remain at Drumlochie House for at least another day.

CHAPTER TWO

JULIA HAD PLENTY to do, for not only did she have to see Mary comfortably settled and work out her diet for the day; there were meals to cook for the five of them as well. Fortunately she was a good cook; at one o'clock she was able to call them into a solid meal of soup, followed by bacon omelettes with jacket potatoes done in the Aga, and a baked rice pudding to follow, and when she would have apologised for the plainness of the fare they looked at her with astonishment, declaring that it was one of the best meals they had eaten for a very long time.

It was after this warming meal that Julia found herself with the doctor while he went over Mary's tests and wrote up the insulin. Mary had responded very well to the penicillin; her chest condition had already improved, although she was sorry enough for herself, but she was too listless to complain about her diet, and for once there seemed no danger of her going into another coma. Julia had given her another penicillin injection at noon and rather to her surprise, her patient had made very little fuss about it and had even laughed a little at the doctor's jokes when he came to see her. Julia stood by him while he wrote up the insulin chart for the rest of the day and as he was putting his pen away, said,

'I—we are very grateful to you, doctor. Mary's better, isn't she?'

'Yes.' He gave her a thoughtful glance. 'Are you in a hurry to be gone?'

'If you mean do I have a job to go to, no. I left St Clare's three days ago—I came here with Mary to oblige her parents—they're abroad, and Matron…'

'You're going on holiday?' He put the question so gently that she answered him without hesitation.

'No, I'm going home to my brother's—his wife—that is, he thinks it would be nice if I stayed with them for a bit and…' She stopped, for she really had no intention of telling him anything about herself. 'Oh, well,' she finished airily, 'it's all arranged,' and if she had expected him to press for more of an answer than that she was disappointed, for all he said was, 'We've dug out the car and ambulance. If it doesn't snow any more today Bert and Willy might get away in the morning.'

Julia was examining what he had written with unnecessary interest.

'Did you mean what you said?' she asked, not looking at him, 'I mean about staying? Don't you have to get home?'

'I can't very well leave my patient, can I?' he wanted to know with an air of reasonableness which she found infuriating. 'I can't deny it's most inconvenient, but then we're all being inconvenienced, aren't we?' He gave her a sideways look. 'Would you like to go for a walk?'

Julia gave him a surprised look and then said sensibly, 'Yes, but I can't—I haven't any boots and I can't leave Mary.'

'We'll get the old retainer to fit you out, and Bert

and Willy can mount guard over Mary for an hour.
You've got to get some fresh air some time.'

She was given no more chance to protest but
caught firmly by the arm and walked back to the
kitchen, where Bert and Willy immediately agreed to
look after their patient and the old man, winkled out
of some cosy haunt of his own, produced rubber boots
which more or less fitted and a great hooded cape
which reached her ankles and had obviously been cut
to fit someone of majestic proportions. The doctor
fastened the hood under her chin with a large safety
pin Bert obligingly produced, got into his own outdoor clothes and opened the back door.

They made their way through the snow and, presently, out of the gate at the back of the garden. It led
on to moorland, which, in the right kind of weather,
must have contained magnificent views. Now only the
nearest of the foot-hills could be seen. The Cheviots,
she knew, were close but shrouded in the still linger-
ing mist into which the trees ahead of them marched,
to disappear into its gloom. 'Do we know where
we're going?' Julia asked with interest.

'Vaguely. We're quite safe as long as it doesn't
snow, and I don't think it will.' He took her arm to
help her along and at the touch of his hand she felt a
little glow of warmth deep inside her.

'It's only three weeks to Christmas,' she observed,
trying to ignore the glow. She would be with her
brother and his family and his friend James would
come over for Christmas dinner. She frowned at the
thought and the doctor said, 'And you're not looking
forward to it.' It was a statement, not a question.

'Well, no, not very, I've spent my last few Christmases in hospital and it was rather fun...'

'But that's not the reason.'

He was far too perceptive. Julia stood still and
looked around her. 'How quiet it is,' she almost whispered. She looked up at the lowering sky too and her
hood fell back. The doctor undid the safety pin and
pulled it back over her black hair, then fastened the
pin again and before she could turn her head away,
bent down and kissed her.

'Only a seasonal greeting,' he explained gravely,
and Julia striving to behave as she felt a sophisticated
young woman should, said a little breathlessly,
'Yes—well, should we be going back?'

He took no notice of this remark but tucked her
hand in his and continued walking through the snow,
while she, hampered by the boots which were a little
on the large side, plodded beside him.

'Tell me about yourself,' he invited, and for a moment she was tempted to do just that—to tell him how
she disliked the idea of going back to Stoke-cum-
Muchelney, because she was afraid that she would
never get away again, only if she married James. She
looked sideways at the man beside her, comparing
him with James, who came off very second best.
James was already getting thin on top, while her companion had plenty of hair on his handsome head, of
a pleasing fairness and elegantly cut; James hadn't a
square chin and his mouth was small and a little thick
in the lip. The doctor had a firm, well-shaped mouth
and his voice was pleasant too, deep and unhurried,
and he didn't say H'm each time he spoke. The
thought that Doctor van den Werff would make the

splendid husband of her vague dreams crossed her mind, to be dismissed immediately. He was a complete stranger—well, almost complete; she knew nothing about him, and, she told herself firmly, she didn't intend to. In a couple of days' time, when the nurse arrived and he could contact the doctor, he would go, and so would she, both to their respective worlds.

'There's nothing to tell,' she replied with a cool politeness which wasn't lost on him, for he said instantly, 'Ah, yes—not my business, eh?'

He let go of her arm and stopped to scoop some snow into his gloved hand, looking at her and laughing as he did so, and she, guessing that the snowball was meant for her, made haste to dodge it, a difficult task with the boots hampering her every step. It would have been silly not to have defended herself, which she did with some success, for he was a large target and although quick on his feet, not quick enough. She tossed the snow at him with all the pleasure of a small child, laughing and shouting and momentarily forgetful of her prosaic future. Presently, still laughing and panting from their exercise, they turned back to the house.

The rest of the day seemed a little dull after that. Julia, her hair tidied once more and crowned with its nurse's cap, returned to her patient, her pink cheeks and sparkling eyes belying the extreme neatness of her person, a fact which Bert and Willy duly remarked upon when she saw them. They had been discussing her, she sensed, as she entered the room, and they made no attempt to hide the fact from her, for Bert said at once,

'We were wondering, Willy and me, if we ought ter go—it don't seem right, leaving you alone. Yer don't mind staying—just with the doc, I mean?'

Julia smiled very nicely at him. 'No,' she said gently, 'I don't mind, Bert. In fact I shall feel quite safe.'

''E seems a nice sort of fellow,' said Willy, 'even though 'e is a foreigner.' He got up and went to the door. 'If yer're quite happy about it, Nurse?'

She answered him seriously. 'If I weren't, Willy, I should have asked you both to stay. What time do you expect to leave in the morning?' She frowned. 'I must write to Sister...'

'Eight o'clock or thereabouts. We'll go back the way we came, though the Carlisle road isn't all that far, but it wouldn't be easy to reach. The doc says he'll come a bit of the way with us, just in case we get stuck. We're going to ring Miss Mary's doctor for him too, so's 'e can come over just as soon as the road's clear. Doc's written it all down for us. I'm to tell 'im you're 'ere as well.'

Julia said uncertainly, 'Oh, are you? I never thought of that.' Nor had she. It seemed Doctor van den Werff had taken the welfare of his fellows very much to heart; she felt pretty certain that when the time came, he would arrange for her departure, buy her ticket and see that she had enough money for necessities on the journey back. Which reminded her, she had a little money with her, but not nearly enough to take her back to London. She would have to borrow, and from the doctor, for it was unthinkable to ask her patient for it and the old retainer was equally impossible. The family doctor might be of help, but she disliked asking for a loan from a stranger. That Doctor van den Werff was a stranger too had for the moment escaped her.

Mary woke up and Julia, who had been standing idly by the window, went to draw up the penicillin before getting her patient's tea and then, when the doctor obligingly said the he would sit with Mary, went down to the vast kitchen to get supper for the rest of them.

She was up early the next morning making sandwiches for the two ambulance men and filling the thermos and then cooking as generous a breakfast as she dared for them. The food was getting a bit low by now, although she would be able to go on making bread for some time, and there were plenty of potatoes, but there was Mary to think of, for as soon as she had recovered from her broncho-pneumonia she would want to eat again. Julia had set aside as much as possible for her, which meant that she and the doctor and Hamish would have to make do with a restricted though ample enough diet.

The morning was a mere glimmer at the end of the long night when she went to the door to see the men off. They wrung her hand, took the letter she had written and trudged through the frozen snow towards the stable. The doctor followed them. He had hardly spoken during breakfast, but now he paused at the door. 'I'll be back as soon as I can,' he said cheerfully, 'but don't worry if I don't turn up until later in the day—we might get held up with the drifts and have to dig ourselves out. If I can get as far as the main road I'll try and find out what's happening about the telephone, or get a message into Hawick. The men will telephone there from Newcastle anyway, but I don't think we should leave any stones unturned, do you?'

Julia asked, 'Will you be able to telephone your family in Holland? Won't they be worrying?' and went faintly pink when he said coolly, 'Time enough for that, Miss Pennyfeather—we have to get you settled first, don't we?'

He grinned suddenly, turned on his heel and set out into the icy morning.

The house was very quiet when they had gone. She had listened to them starting up the ambulance and then the car and, minutes later, their horns blaring a goodbye to her as the noise of the engines became fainter and fainter and then ceased altogether, leaving her lonely.

But there wasn't much time for loneliness; there was Mary to see to and the rooms to tidy and the food cupboard to be frowned over once more. Hamish had brought in some more eggs, but everything else was getting on the low side, though there was plenty if someone arrived that evening and brought food with them, but Julia had looked out of the window as soon as it was light and had been disquieted by the grey sky with its ominous yellow tinges streaking the horizon, and the wind was getting up again as well. She went back to Mary's room and built up a magnificent fire as though by so doing she could ward off the bad weather she guessed was coming.

The wind began to whine in real earnest about three o'clock and the first snowflakes whirled down, slowly and daintily at first and then in real earnest. It didn't look as though the nurse would arrive that day, nor the cook and the maid, nor, for that matter, thought Julia gloomily, Doctor van den Werff. He was probably stuck in some drift miles from anywhere; she was thankful that she had made him take some sandwiches and a thermos too.

She took Mary's tea up presently, to find her awake and more cheerful, and she was still with her when she heard the car return. It was dark outside and the fast falling snow almost obliterated its headlights as it went past the house in the direction of the stables. Julia left Mary to finish her tea and went downstairs, her cape held close against the draughts, and reached the kitchen as the doctor came in from outside, bringing a rush of cold air in with him.

Julia went to the stove and opened one of the plates so that the singing kettle could boil. 'I thought you'd never get here,' she said, trying to make her voice light.

The doctor took off his coat and shook a quantity of snow from it on to the floor, then hung it on the back of a chair where it began to steam. Only then did he speak, and the extreme placidity of his voice annoyed her.

'My dear Miss Pennyfeather,' he remarked, 'I told you that I should come,' which calm and brief speech caused her to burst out, 'Well, I know you did, but sitting here waiting for you isn't the same...'

'Waiting for me, were you? I'm flattered—at least I should have been in any other circumstances. Unfortunately the telephone wires are still down—I wasted a great deal of time. Still, the snow ploughs have been out on the main road.' He sat down at the table and she realised that this meagre information was all she was going to get about his day. She poured him some tea from the pot she had just made and offered him bread and jam.

'Is the weather very bad?' she wanted to know.

'Quite nasty, but I don't fancy it's going to last. Has everything been all right here?' He glanced at Hamish, who nodded before Julia could answer. 'Aye, the fires are lit, and there's plenty of wood. I'll kill a chicken tomorrow.'

The doctor nodded. 'Good idea—otherwise I'll have to go out with a gun.'

'What,' said Julia indignantly, 'and shoot any small creature, half-starved and frozen?'

He didn't laugh at her. 'I shouldn't enjoy it,' he said gently, 'but we have to eat. But don't worry, if Hamish here lets us have a chicken we'll do very well for a couple of days—Mary can have it too.'

Julia agreed, wondering the while what Mary's mother would say when she arrived home and found no food in the cupboards and several beds in use. But of course they would all be gone by then and she herself would never know, she would be in Somerset and this strange adventure would be a dream—so would the doctor. She sighed and got up to refill the teapot.

She had tucked Mary up for the night and had gone to her room to sit by the fire before beginning the chilly business of undressing when there was a knock on the door and the doctor came in.

'Mary?' asked Julia as she started to her feet.

'No—she's asleep, I've just been to look. I want to talk to you and your room is warmer than mine—do you mind if I come in?'

Julia felt surprise, pleasure and finally a faint ex-
citement which she firmly suppressed. She sat down
again. 'There's a chair in that corner, it's larger than
the others,' she said sensibly.

His lips twitched, but he went obediently and
fetched it, sat down opposite her and began without
preamble.

'The reason I was going to London before returning
to Holland was in order that I might engage a nurse
to take back with me. There is a young lady staying
with my family—an English girl who contracted polio
just before I came over to Edinburgh. She went to
hospital, of course, but now she is back with us, but
I hear that she is very bored with only my sister to
talk to, for she doesn't care to learn Dutch. She's
convalescent and has made a splendid recovery which
I feel could be hastened even more by having someone with her to whom she could talk freely.'

He paused and looked across at Julia, his eyebrows
lifted in an unspoken question.

'Me?' asked Julia, and felt a pleasant tingle of ex-
citement.

'Yes—it would save me hunting around in London,
and I think that you may suit admirably. You are very
much of an age and capable with it. If you could see
your way to coming for a few weeks? I know it is
sudden, but I fancy you wouldn't mind overmuch if
you didn't go to your brother's. Am I right?'

'Yes—I don't want to go in the least,' she said
bluntly, 'but I really should.'

'Forgive me, but is your brother not able to afford
a nurse for his wife, or help of some sort?'

She flushed. 'Yes, of course he can, only I expect

he feels it's a waste of money to pay someone when there's me.'

'So you would have no feeling of—er—guilt if you were not to go?'

Julia was a little surprised to find that she didn't feel in the least guilty. She said briefly, 'No.'

'Then, Miss Pennyfeather, will you come? I know this is a most irregular way of offering a job, but in the rather peculiar circumstances in which we find ourselves...you trust me?'

Julia looked startled. 'Trust you? Of course I trust you.' Her voice sounded as startled as her face. 'I hope I shall suit your patient.'

She hoped that he might give her a few more details, but it seemed that he didn't intend doing so, not at that moment anyway, for he went on to ask her if she had a passport and would she mind being out of England for Christmas.

She said a little breathlessly, for she was still surprised at herself for her rash acceptance of a job she knew nothing about, 'Yes—I've a passport, it's with my things in London. I've never been out of England at Christmas time, but I don't suppose I shall mind.'

'No? I daresay you'll find it much the same as in England. We have the same family gatherings, but I don't think we put quite such emphasis on presents. We have St Nikolaas, you see, earlier in the month.'

She nodded, having only a slight inkling of what he was talking about. She had heard of St Nikolaas, naturally, and she knew all about his white horse and Black Peter, but that was already over and done with; it was almost Christmas. A Christmas she might enjoy much more than if she went to her brother's.

His voice cut through her thoughts with a gentle persistence she couldn't ignore. 'If I might have your attention, Miss Pennyfeather? We shall have to stay here until such time as the nurse, the doctor and the servants arrive, then I propose to drive down to London where you can collect your clothes and whatever else you want. We can cross from Harwich when it suits us and drive home from there.'

Julia watched him put another log on the fire. 'I don't know where you live.'

'Near Tilburg, a small town called Oisterwijk. I work at the hospital in Tilburg—I'm an anaesthetist. I also go once a week to Breda and s'Hertogenbosch and occasionally to Eindhoven. My father has a practice in which I am a partner and when he retires I shall take it over. My sister runs the household and I have two brothers younger than I—one is married, the youngest is still finishing his post-graduate course at a Utrecht hospital.'

'And my patient?'

He gave her a sharp glance and took so long in replying that she thought that probably he was deciding what to tell her. 'Miss Marcia Jason,' he said at length, 'who was staying with us when she was taken ill. We are all very fond of her, and to get her completely well again is our dearest wish.'

Julia ignored the pang she felt at his words, for she suspected that it had something to do with the doctor being fond of his patient... It was extremely foolish of her to get interested in him. She told herself that it was only because they had been thrown together in trying circumstances that she felt...she decided not to pursue her train of thought and looked up to see the doctor regarding her steadily. 'And now,' he invited, 'tell me something of yourself.'

To her surprise she did, although she hadn't really meant to. Out it all came, her brother and Maureen and her home and how lovely the garden was in the summer and how awful London was if you hadn't anywhere to go—and James. He didn't speak, just sat and listened as she enlarged upon James and his tedious perfections. 'He's s-so right always,' she ended, 'and so dreadfully patient and good when I lose my temper. He says I'll be better when we settle down: But I don't want to settle down—not with him.'

'Have you anyone in mind?' queried her companion mildly.

She said uncertainly, 'No—oh, no,' and knew in her heart that it wasn't quite true. James and Maureen and her brother too had told her a great many times that there was no such thing as love at first sight; love came gradually, they had explained patiently, and Julia, an unwilling listener, had considered that it all sounded rather dull. She had said so, passionately, and they had smiled at her with pitying coolness. She said now, 'I shouldn't have said all that about James.' She gave the doctor a direct look. 'It was disloyal.'

He smiled nicely. 'No. As far as I can judge, you owe this James nothing, and you can be sure that I'll forget everything about the tiresome fellow, and I suggest that you do too, otherwise you'll find yourself living in a semi-detached with a great deal to do and a string of babies.'

'But I like babies!'

He closed his eyes. 'So do I, Miss Pennyfeather. How delightful that we agree upon such an important

aspect of life. If we persevere we shall undoubtedly
find other things just as important.'

Julia stared at him, her lovely eyes wide. As though
it mattered if they agreed about anything! The fewer
things the better, she was inclined to think, bearing
in mind Miss Marcia Jason...

'Is she pretty?' she asked suddenly. The doctor
looked as though he was laughing silently, but he had
that sort of face, anyway.

'Very,' he answered without hesitation, 'small and
fair, with large blue eyes. She has an extremely intelligent brain.'

'Has the polio affected her badly?'

'Luckily the damage is slight. It's a question of
constant encouragement, that's why I thought a nurse,
someone sensible and her own age, would give her
the stimulus she needs for the last few weeks of con-
valescence.'

Julia nodded while she seethed. She had had her
share of men friends, none of whom had ever called
her sensible in that matter-of-fact voice. She gave him
a cross look and went scarlet when he added, 'Not
that being sensible is your only attribute, my dear
young lady, but it is the only one which applies in
this case, I think.' He got up, taking his time, and at
the door he said, 'Let us pray for good weather so
that we may get away from here as soon as possible;
I have never suffered so many draughts. Goodnight,
Miss Pennyfeather.'

It snowed again the next day, but late in the afternoon the weathered cleared and at teatime Hamish
offered the information that the worst was over, and
neither Julia nor Doctor van den Werff thought to

question his pronouncement, for after all, he had lived in the Border country all his life, and he should know. As if to bear him out the radio in the doctor's car proclaimed exactly the same state of affairs, if in somewhat more elaborate language, adding a rider to the effect that telephone communications were being reinstated as quickly as possible. But the telephone at Drumlochie House remained silent and no one arrived, which wasn't surprising, for the snow plough hadn't got so far.

The snow plough, however, came the next morning and Doctor van den Werff went up to the road and brought the driver back for coffee. The road was clear, the man told them, at least a narrow lane of it, and once on the main road the going wasn't too bad, although he warned them about skidding and went on to relate, to the delight of old Hamish, several unfortunate incidents which had occurred owing to the bad weather; he would have gone on for some time in like vein had not the doctor reminded him that he still had the stretch of road to Hawick to clear. When he had gone the doctor looked at his watch and remarked. 'He should be there by midday or a little after. I should think we might expect someone by this evening. It is to be hoped that the telephone will be working again before then so that I can talk to Mary's doctor—he should have had my message by now, that is, if Bert managed to get it to him.'

The doctor didn't telephone, but came in his car with Jane and Madge sitting inside it. By the look on their faces, Julia thought that perhaps the journey hadn't been all that smooth, a supposition the doctor bore out with forceful language when he got out of the car. 'But I got your message,' he said as he looked round the hall for Doctor van den Werff, who wasn't there, 'and I came as soon as I could—I had no idea...is Mary all right?'

Julia, easing him out of his duffle coat, said that yes, she believed so and that Doctor van den Werff would have heard the car and would be in to tell him all he wished to know. She then offered everyone tea, introduced herself to Jane and Madge, begged them to go and get warm in the kitchen and then inquired of the doctor if he had brought any food with him.

'In the boot, I'll bring it in presently, Nurse.' He turned away as Doctor van den Werff walked in and Julia made her escape, leaving them to introduce themselves, for she had no idea of the doctor's name.

They were drinking tea while Julia apologised for the amount of food they had eaten during their stay, when the two men came in with the air of people who were quite satisfied with each other. She poured them each a cup, offered a plate of scones and murmuring something about seeing to Mary, went upstairs, followed almost immediately by Jane and Madge, who made much of the invalid and listened with patience to her highly coloured version of her journey home. They rose to go at length, promising supper within a couple of hours, and went away, discussing the merits of a nice toad-in-the-hole as opposed to Quiche Lorraine. Scarcely had they gone when the two doctors presented themselves at the door and spent half an hour examining their patient and studying charts after which her own doctor pronounced himself well satisfied as to her condition and promised to be out the following morning. 'And the nurse,' he observed, 'I fancy she'll be here very shortly,' he smiled at Julia. 'You'll be free to go, Nurse, with my grateful thanks.'

Julia murmured a reply, thankful that she had made up the bed in the room next to hers. She would get someone to light a fire there as soon as possible. The doctor shook her hand in a powerful grip, thanked her once more and went downstairs. Presently she heard his car making its careful way back to the road.

When she went downstairs presently the doctor was nowhere to be seen, but when she went into the hall she heard his voice in the sitting room, an icy apartment which housed the telephone which she was pleased to see he was using. He looked up as she went in and said cheerfully,

'We're on again, and the wind has brought back the electric too.' He got up and came towards her. 'What do you think of Doctor MacIntory?'

Julia looked at him, her head a little on one side. 'He seemed very nice—so that's his name. Do you plan to go tomorrow if the nurse comes tonight?'

He nodded. 'If you have no objection, I'm anxious to get home.' He smiled suddenly and because his smile gave her a faintly lightheaded sensation, she said the first thing which came into her head. 'What sort of car have you got?' she wanted to know.

'Come and see,' he invited, and went to fetch the cloak hanging behind the kitchen door and wrapped her in it and gave her his hand to hold because the steps were ice-covered again. The stable was gloomy and cold and could have housed half a dozen motor cars; there was only one there now—the doctor's and well worth housing. It was a Jensen Interceptor, gleaming and sleek and powerful. She walked round it exclaiming, 'What a lovely car—how fast does she go?'

He laughed. 'Just over a hundred and thirty miles an hour, but we'll be lucky if we manage fifty in this weather.'

Julia withdrew her head from the interior of the car and turned to look at him. She said politely, 'Look, I'm sure you're anxious to be gone. Would you like to go now? There's nothing to keep you, you've seen the doctor and done more than you need...the nurse might not come...I can go back by train.'

She got no further, for the doctor had her by the shoulders and was shaking her gently. 'I have no patience with you,' he said a trifle testily. 'Of course I'm anxious to get home, but you don't really think that I would go just like that and leave you here? Besides, I like company on a long journey and I should have to wait for you in London.' His hands tightened on her shoulders as he bent his head to kiss her. 'Have you forgotten, Julia, that I've engaged you to look after Marcia?'

Being kissed like that had made her forget everything, but it didn't seem very wise to say so. She withdrew a little from him and said in a commendably sensible voice, 'No, of course I hadn't.' A very large image of the beautiful Miss Jason floated before her eyes. She said firmly, 'I think I must go and see how Mary...' then paused, frowning. 'I can hear...there's a cat here,' she said quickly. 'Oh, the poor thing!'

The doctor went past her to a corner of the stable. 'Yes, there is,' he said casually. 'At least, there are five—mother and kittens—look!'

Julia peered down into the apple box filled with

straw which he indicated, and the mother cat, with the kittens crawling around her, peered back. Julia said in a voice soft with pity, 'Oh, please can't we take them inside and feed them?'

'She's the stable cat and won't stay in the house. I found the box for her before the kittens arrived and I've fed her regularly. She's fine. I'll tell Jane or Madge to keep an eye on them when we go.'

Julia stooped and put out a finger, and the cat licked it politely and then turned to the more urgent business of washing her kittens. Julia stood up and looked at her companion. 'You're very kind. A lot of men wouldn't have bothered,' she said. 'Why didn't you tell me? I could have fed her.'

'You had enough to do. You're a practical young woman, aren't you, Julia?'

Part of her mind registered the pleasing fact that he had called her Julia twice within a few minutes while she replied, 'I don't know—I suppose being in hospital makes one practical.' She started walking towards the door. 'Do you think the nurse will come today? It's already five o'clock and very dark.'

The doctor opened the stable door before he replied. The wind was slight but icy cold and Julia shivered and wrapped her voluminous cape more closely round her as they made their way back to the house.

'I should think the trains are running,' said the doctor. 'She's coming straight from Edinburgh to Hawick and if the doctor could get through so can a taxi.'

It seemed his words were to be ratified. Barely an hour later a car rolled to a halt at the front door. Julia heard it from Mary's room where she was doing the evening chores, and hurried downstairs to welcome the arrival, but Doctor van den Werff had heard the taxi too and was already there, talking to a small woman, who could have been any age from forty to fifty, and whose pleasant face lighted up with a smile when she saw Julia. The doctor performed the introductions smoothly, giving them barely time to utter the most commonplace civilities before suggesting that the kitchen might be a warmer place than the draughty hall.

'Oh, how thoughtless of me,' cried Julia, 'you and the driver must be frozen!' She led the way to the kitchen. 'I'm sure Jane won't mind if I make you some tea.' She arranged Miss MacBonar on one side of the stove and the driver on the other and went to where Jane was making pastry at the table.

'You don't mind,' she begged that lady, 'if they sit here get warm, and would you mind very much if I made them some tea? I'm afraid we've used the kitchen to live in while you've been away.'

Jane smiled. 'Aye, it's a cold house, Nurse—it's been none too easy for you, I daresay. And don't worry about the tea. Madge made it when she heard the taxi. Should I keep the driver here for his supper, do you think? It'll be easier going on the way home if he's got something hot inside him.'

'What a good idea. I'm going back to Miss Mary now and then I'll come back and take Miss MacBonar up to meet her. I expect you know that the doctor and I are leaving tomorrow?'

Madge gave her a quick glance. 'Aye, he told me. A kind gentleman he is, ye'll have a safe journey with him.'

Julia said a little shyly, 'Yes, I'm sure I shall,' and

made her way through the icy hall and up the stairs to Mary, who was sitting up in her chair by the fire, demanding to know exactly what the new nurse was like.

'Nice,' said Julia promptly. 'If I were ill I should like her to nurse me—I'm going to fetch her in a few minutes and then I'll get your supper and take her down to have supper with us.' She picked up the insulin syringe. 'Now roll up your sleeve, Mary—it's time for your injection.'

Nurse MacBonar and Mary took to each other on sight; Julia left them together while she went down for Mary's tray and having settled that young lady to her satisfaction, took her colleague along to her own room to give her the details of her patient. 'And your room's next door,' she explained, 'and I'm sure if you don't like it no one will mind if you change. I'm afraid we just took the first ones we saw when we arrived. There's a fire going and I've put a hot water bottle in the bed. I wondered if you would like half an hour to yourself until supper? I'll come and fetch you.'

They went downstairs together a little later to find that the table had been laid in the dining room, a forbidding apartment with a great many hunting trophies on its walls and a quantity of heavy mahogany furniture arranged very stiffly beneath them. But there was a fire in the hearth and the supper was ample and well cooked. The three of them sat at one end of the large oval table and Nurse MacBonar told them at some length and a good deal of dry humour of her difficulties in reaching them.

'But I hear from Doctor MacIntory that you had

your ups and downs too,' she remarked cheerfully. 'I can imagine how you felt when you arrived,' she looked at them in turn. 'Did you get here to together?'

It was the doctor who answered. 'No, for I am on my way to London from Edinburgh—I got hopelessly lost, and how I got here I have no idea, but Miss Pennyfeather was kind enough to take me in...'

'Weren't you scared?' inquired Miss MacBonar of Julia. 'A strange man coming to the door like that?'

Julia avoided the doctor's eyes. 'I was so cold and tired I didn't think about it,' she confessed, 'otherwise I daresay I should have been frightened.'

'Oh well,' said Miss MacBonar comfortably, 'it was only the doctor here, so there was no need.'

This time Julia glanced up to find him watching her and although his face showed nothing of it, she knew that he was laughing silently. He said pleasantly, 'You invest me with a character I fear I cannot lay claim to. Miss Pennyfeather, who has had to put up with me these last few days, could tell you how tiresome I can be at times.'

Nurse MacBonar chuckled. 'Aren't all men tiresome at some time or another?' she wanted to know. 'Not that the world would be much of a place without them, and I should know—I've buried two husbands. Are either of you married?'

Julia shook her head and the doctor murmured in a negative manner.

'Ah, well, your turn will come. Do you plan to leave early?'

Doctor van den Werff picked up his fork preparatory to demolishing the portion of bread and butter pudding Julia had just handed to him.

'Eight o'clock—that will allow for any small hold-ups on the way.' He looked at Julia with lifted brows. 'That is if our Miss Pennyfeather is agreeable?'

Julia, smouldering inwardly at being addressed as our Miss Pennyfeather, said coolly, 'Yes, quite, thank you,' and then addressed herself to Miss MacBonar. 'I'll call you before I go, shall I? Mary sleeps until eight or thereabouts, so you'll have plenty of time to dress.'

They separated to go their various ways after supper. Julia to get Mary into bed and settled for the night.

She was a little silent as she went quiet-footed about the room putting everything to rights. Her patient lay watching her and then asked, 'Aren't you excited about tomorrow? Lucky you—all day with Ivo.'

'Ivo?' asked Julia.

'Doctor van den Werff, silly. Isn't it a nice name? I like him, don't you?'

Julia, looking for a clean nightie for her patient, agreed. 'Oh, yes, and you have cause to be grateful to him too.'

'Well, I am. I told him so. I'm grateful to you too. Have I been a good patient?'

Julia looked across the room at her charge, a little wan still but pretty for all that. She said generously, 'Yes, you have. It hasn't been much fun for you, has it, but you've stuck to your diet like a brick and not fussed over your injections. Go on being good, won't you? Nurse MacBonar is nice, don't you think? We both like her very much and she'll look after you splendidly, and if you keep to your diet and do as you're told you'll be able to lead the same life as any of your friends.'

'Yes, Ivo told me that too. I'll try. I like you, Nurse Pennyfeather—I like Ivo too. You'd make a handsome pair.' She narrowed her blue eyes and stared at Julia, who stared back, mouth agape.

'We'd what?' Julia reiterated.

'Make an awfully handsome pair. I can just see you coming down the aisle together, you with your eyes sparkling like they do when you're pleased and happy and your cheeks all pink, and him, proud and smiling.'

Julia contrived a laugh, a very natural one considering her heart leapt into her throat and was choking her. She said with admirable calm, 'Go on with you, Mary, it's your own wedding you should be thinking about, not anyone else's. Now go to sleep, because I shall wake you early to say goodbye in the morning.'

They wished each other goodnight and Julia, as it was still early, went along to Miss MacBonar's room, trying to dismiss Mary's words from her mind and failing utterly.

Her colleague had finished unpacking and had arranged her small possessions around her so that the room looked almost cosy. She looked up as Julia knocked and went in and said, 'There you are, dear. Should we go down and have a last word with the doctor? I think he expects it.'

Julia ran a finger along the carved back of the rather uncomfortable chair she was leaning against. 'He doesn't expect me,' she said positively, 'but I'm sure he'd like to see you—last-minute things,' she added vaguely. 'Doctor MacIntory said he'd be along tomorrow if we've forgotten anything. The charts are in the table drawer in Mary's room, and I've brought the insulin and syringe with me—I keep them in my room, here they are.'

She handed them over and Nurse MacBonar nodded understandingly and got to her feet. 'Then I'll pop along then and see that nice doctor of yours.' She beamed at Julia as they went out of the room together. 'You won't come too?'

'No, I don't think so. I'm tired,' said Julia mendaciously. They wished each other goodnight and she went along to her room and started to undress slowly, oblivious of the room's chill. She wasn't tired at all. There was no reason at all why she shouldn't have gone downstairs with Nurse MacBonar, at least no reason she was prepared to admit, even to herself.

CHAPTER THREE

IT WAS COLD and dark when they left the next morning after the ample breakfast Madge had insisted upon them eating. And the road was like a skating rink. Julia clutched her hands tightly together under her cloak, sitting very stiff and upright beside the doctor, expecting every minute to go off the road or land upside down in a ditch.

'Sit back,' commanded her companion quietly, 'nothing's going to happen. You aren't frightened?'

'I'm terrified!' declared Julia.

'You must have realised that it would be like this?'

'Yes, of course I did.' She spoke crossly.

'And yet you came with me?'

'Well, I—I'm sure you're a good driver,' she answered lamely.

'So you trust me as a driver as well. Good. Go on trusting me, Julia. Lean your head back and relax—I shan't take any risks.'

She did as she was told and found to her surprise that after a little while she was actually enjoying the nightmare journey in an apprehensive sort of way, and when presently the doctor asked her if she was warm enough and then went on to talk about a hundred and one unimportant things, his quiet voice never altering its placid tones, flowing on through even the most hair-raising skids, she found herself answering him in a quite natural voice, and if her lovely face was a little paler than usual, there was no one to remark upon it.

Once on the main road the going was easier, although woefully slow in places so that when they reached Newcastle the doctor judged it wise to order sandwiches with their coffee in case it might prove difficult to stop later on.

The M1, when they got to it, was almost clear of snow, however, although lumps of it, frozen solid, added to the hazards of the already icy surface, but traffic was sparse at first and there was no fog so that they made good progress; so much so that south of Doncaster the doctor suggested that they should stop for lunch.

'There's a place I've been to before,' he said, 'a mile or two off the motorway. I think it's called Bawtry.'

It was pleasant to get off the monotonous highway for just a little while, and the old coaching inn where he stopped looked inviting.

'I'm sorry about my uniform,' said Julia as they went inside. 'I don't look very glamorous.'

He gave her a sideways glance. 'And what makes you think that I like a glamorous companion?'

She said in a prosaic voice, 'I thought men did.'

He took her arm because the pavement was still slippery. 'Not always,' he said, half laughing, 'in any case you've no need to worry; with your looks you could get away with anything you choose to put on.'

He said it so carelessly that she felt doubtful if he meant it as a compliment. She sighed and he said at once, 'You're tired, you need a meal.'

The food was good and the dining room pleasantly

warm. They ate roast beef with all its traditional accompaniments washed down with burgundy, and while the doctor contented himself with the cheese board, Julia, who had a sweet tooth, applied herself to a chocolate soufflé. She ate with relish and as she put down her fork, remarked, 'You know, food you haven't cooked yourself always tastes different—besides, we had rather a monotonous diet at Drumlochie House, didn't we?'

'But excellently cooked. We were all glad there was no bread, yours was so delicious.'

'I enjoyed baking it,' said Julia simply. 'What time shall we get to London?'

'Almost a hundred and sixty miles—it's hard to say. Three hours normally, but I should think we might double that allowing for slow going and holdups. Getting bored?' he asked with a smile.

Julia shook her head, wishing very much to tell him that she was enjoying every minute of his company. Instead she remarked, 'Not in the least. I like motoring, though I don't do so much of it.'

'Hasn't James got a car?'

She pinkened. 'Yes—a Morris, but he doesn't believe that you should travel fast on the roads nor that you should use a car solely for pleasure.'

The doctor choked. 'Good God—what kind of pleasure?'

'Well, short trips to the sea, somewhere where we could do the shopping at the same time, and—and picnics…'

'Sandwiches and a thermos flask?' he wanted to know.

'Yes. James considers eating out is a great waste

of money.' Her already pink cheeks went a little pinker. 'Oh, I beg your pardon, that sounds rude and ungrateful just after you've given me such a gorgeous lunch. I—I didn't mean that at all; I love eating out and driving miles. I'd forgotten what fun it was.' She sounded wistful.

'I can see that I shall have to rescue you from James.'

'How?'

'By a method which will prove quite infallible.' The doctor's voice was light. Julia decided that he was joking. She asked equally lightly,

'Do tell me.'

He shook his head, 'No—not yet, but I promise it will work.'

They got up to go and Julia, still persisting, asked, 'You mean if I take a job away from home for a long time he might forget me?'

'Something like that.'

The short winter's day was already dimming although it was barely two o'clock. Julia looked anxiously at the sky as they got into the car. 'It's not going to snow again, is it?' she asked worriedly.

'I shouldn't think so. If it does and it gets too bad we'll just have to stay the night somewhere, but I don't think that will he necessary.'

She settled down as he started the car, drawing her cloak around her, thankful for the warmth and comfort. Presently she closed her eyes; they were back on the M1 once more and there was nothing to see, only the road running ahead of them and the traffic weaving in and out of the lanes in a never-ending, tiring pattern. The doctor was doing a steady fifty, overtaking whenever he had the opportunity; he didn't seem disposed to talk. She opened her eyes and peeped at him once; his good-looking profile looked stern and thoughtful. Immersed in dreams of Miss Marcia Jason, thought Julia pettishly, and closed her eyes again, sternly dismissing her own dreams. She opened them a few moments later, aware of something wrong, although the man beside her had made no sound. They were on the point of passing an articulated lorry and as she looked behind her the doctor accelerated to a sudden breathtaking speed, sliding ahead of it with seconds to spare as a car, roaring down the motorway, passed them within inches. Julia caught a glimpse of its occupants laughing and waving. 'That was a bit near,' she said in a voice which quavered just a little. 'I'm glad you're a good driver.'

The doctor sounded grim. 'Yes, so am I—they're the sort who cause a pile-up. He passed us at over a hundred and twenty.'

'What were we doing when you overtook?' Julia wanted to know.

He grinned. 'Never you mind,' he replied, 'but it was either that or being pushed into the next world...' He broke off and said something harsh and sudden in his own language, and Julia watched with silent horror as the car, careering madly half a mile ahead of them, tried to pass a huge transport which was on the point of crossing into the fast lane, and even as she watched she was aware that the doctor had slowed and was edging back on to the slow lane and on to the hard shoulder of the road, to stop close to the appalling chaos.

The transport driver, in a last-minute attempt to

avert disaster, had slewed to his left, but the oncoming car had been too fast for him. It was wedged, no longer recognisable as a car, under the huge back wheels, its recent occupants lying untidily around it. Even as they were looking, two more cars crashed into it.

The doctor reached across Julia, locked the door and undid her safety belt. 'When I get out,' he commanded, 'get into my seat and don't put a foot outside the door until I say so.'

He took his bag from the back seat and got out himself, and then after a quick look around, turned to help her. The traffic, for the most part, was still moving south down the slow lane, Julia could hear the urgent squeak of brakes behind them as they made their way to the wrecked cars. There was already a small crowd of people—the doctor tapped the nearest man on the shoulder and said with mild authority,

'Would you go to the side of the motorway and find the telephone? One shouldn't be too far away—tell the police and say we shall want several ambulances.' He didn't wait to see if the man would do as he asked but shouldered his way through the little group, propelling Julia along beside him. The first victim lay very quietly, which was only to be expected of someone with a compound fracture of skull and a badly torn leg. Doctor van den Werff examined her swiftly, grunted gently and said, 'Get a tourniquet on that leg, Julia, and try and get a pad and some sort of bandage on her head, then come to me.' He opened his case, gave her a handful of slings and a packet of gauze and went away.

Once she had something to do, it wasn't so bad.

Julia forgot the horror of it all in the urgency of her work. She begged a tie off a man standing nearby, tightened her home-made torniquet with her pen and then turned her attention to the woman's head. There wasn't a great deal which could be done. She covered the wounds carefully with gauze and slid a cotton sling carefully around the woman's head and fastened it loosely, then enlisted the tieless man's help, explaining what he had to do about the tourniquet, and went to find the doctor.

He was sprawled across the wreckage of the first car, his head and shoulders out of sight in the tangle of twisted steel; she worked her way to his side and looked inside too. Her almost soundless 'Oh' was full of horror and she closed her eyes, willing herself not to be sick. She opened them again as the doctor pulled her out to stand beside him. He said in a perfectly ordinary voice, 'Very nasty, but I doubt if he knew anything about it. Who's next?'

Julia, her face very white, spoke with a mouth which shook a little.

'That woman—I left a man with her, he seemed sensible. There's someone screaming...'

'Hysterics,' said the doctor briefly. 'Let's have a look at this one.' A man this time, conscious and miraculously only slightly injured. The doctor sent him to the side of the road, accompanied by two willing helpers, who, now that they had got over the initial shock, had offered, as had several others, to help in any way they could. The next one was a man too, with a leg twisted at a strange angle and a pale, unconscious face. The doctor felt the man's head with gentle fingers and said,

'I think we'll leave him as he is until the ambulances get here. But we'll splint that leg.'

Which he did, with the aid of two planks of wood torn from a packing case and two more ties. Two children came next, both sadly dead. Julia turned away from them with a heavy heart to join the doctor at the side of the last victim—a woman, and conscious. Her pale lips sketched a smile as they knelt down beside her. 'It's my back,' she whispered, 'it feels funny.'

The doctor said with gentle decisiveness, 'They'll put that right in hospital. Stay exactly as you are, will you, my dear? You'll not have to wait long, I can hear the ambulance now.'

He stayed where he was, a gentle hand on her shoulder, and said to Julia, 'Tell the ambulance men to come to this patient first and fast. Then find the driver of the transport—he's not amongst this lot, probably he's all right, just shocked, and if I'm not about see if anyone was hurt in the other two cars. I don't think so, they'd all better be examined in hospital.'

Julia sped away, glad to have something to do. The driver was still sitting in his cab, dazed with shock and but for a few bruises, unhurt. All the same, she persuaded him to go with her in search of the doctor, whom she found helping to load the woman with the broken back on to an ambulance. He gave her a hasty glance. 'He's all right? Leave him here, I'll have a quick look before he goes for a check-up. See about the others?'

She saw about them; bruises and a cut or two and some nasty grazes, nothing that half an hour in hos-

pital casualty wouldn't put right. She led them, un-
naturally quiet with shock, over to the ambulances too
and sat them on the blankets someone had spread on
the grass at the side of the road, then looked for the
doctor. He was with the group of police and ambulance men and a breakdown lorry gang, bending over
the wreckage where the dead man lay. She looked
away as they began to draw something covered in a
blanket out of the tangled mess, her stomach turning
over, and most fortunately had her attention immediately distracted by the arrival of another ambulance,
complete with doctor and nurse. By the time she had
answered their immediate questions, the little group
had dispersed from around the wrecked car and Doctor van den Werff was wiping his hands on a towel
produced by one of the ambulance men, and while he
talked to the doctor Julia went with the nurse to see
what help they might give the ambulance men in
stowing the remainder of the slightly injured passen-
gers into the last two ambulances, but she had only
been with them a very few minutes when the doctor
tapped her on the shoulder, picked up his car coat
from the ground where he had tossed it earlier and
instead of putting it on, draped it around her shoulders; it was only as he did so that she discovered that
she was shivering violently. They had reached the car
when she said in a surprised, tight little voice, 'I think
I'm going to faint,' and did so.

She came round in the car, with her cap off and
her head against the doctor's shoulder, as she opened
her eyes he said mildly,

'Stay as you are,' and she was glad to do so; his
shoulder felt comfortably solid under her swimming

head and the weight of his arm round her shoulders was reassuring.

'I've never done that before,' she said in a surprised apologetic voice. 'That man in the car...'

His arm tightened. 'Forget him,' his voice was calm and matter-of-fact and very kind. 'Think instead of the help you were able to give to the others.'

'I didn't do much,' she said forlornly, almost on the verge of tears. 'You did all the work...those two children...'

He ignored her last muttered words and said briskly, 'If you hadn't helped me I should have wasted a great deal of time bandaging and tying splints and so forth, and while I was doing that someone else might have died.'

'The man in the car, and the children...do you think they...?'

If he felt impatience at her insistence he gave no sign but said in his calm way, 'None of them knew anything about it, and that's the truth, Julia; you're too nice a person to lie to.'

For some reason Julia couldn't even guess at, she began to cry then. She cried and snivelled and sniffed while the doctor sat silent, and when at last she fumbled for her handkerchief, he offered her his own, still without speaking.

Her face mopped, she sat up, feeling a great deal better, and made shift to repair the damage to her face and tidy her hair, still sniffing from time to time. When she had finished her eyes still looked red and so did the tip of her nose, but neither of these things could dim her vivid good looks. She said soberly, 'If you want to change your mind about employing me to look after Miss Jason, I shall quite understand.'

He looked completely taken aback. 'But I don't want to change my mind. Whatever put the idea into your head? I want only the best for Marcia, and I think you are exactly what I hoped to find.' His voice was very decided and Julia heaved a sigh of relief.

'Oh, thank you—I thought I'd better ask after making such a fool of myself. Have you a very deep regard for her?'

She heard him sigh, but all he said was: 'I haven't seen her for six months.' Which didn't quite answer her question. He had sighed very deeply, though; Julia, who had a romantic nature, thought that it was probably with longing. She quelled a fresh desire to burst into tears once more, although for quite a different reason this time, and when he suggested that they should stop for tea at the earliest opportunity, she was able to agree in a calm little voice which was, nevertheless, quite unlike her usual tones.

The accident had occurred a few miles north of Nottingham. The doctor started the car and drove past the chaos. He was going faster now despite the icy road, but there was no fault to find with his driving; Julia sat back relaxed in a friendly silence until a sudden thought struck her and she asked,

'Have you somewhere to go tonight? Will it be a little late for you to go to a hotel?'

She could not see his face, but she was sure that he was smiling.

'I think I shall be all right—I usually go to the same hotel when I'm in London—they know me there. What about you? Your friend will be home?'

'I'm sure she will, and even if she isn't I know where the second key is hidden.' She added shyly, 'I'm sure she'll be glad to give you a meal.'

'That's kind, but I believe I'll go straight to the hotel when I've seen you safely there. I want to telephone to Holland.'

Miss Jason, thought Julia sadly. How he must dote on her to telephone her all that way at that time of night! She wondered what it would feel like to be loved like that and was unable to pursue the thought further because he was speaking again. 'I'll come round and see you some time tomorrow if I may. Do you suppose you could be ready to catch the night boat from Harwich?'

'Yes, of course, I've only to pack a few things.' She stared ahead of her into the dark night, made darker by the car's powerful lights, aware that if he had asked her to go with him to the other side of the world she would have given him the same reply because she loved him; she admitted the fact to herself without surprise and with the unhappy satisfaction of knowing that her brother and Maureen and James had all been wrong—love for her, at least, hadn't come gradually. It had come when she had opened a door to a stranger on a bitter cold night.

They reached Connie's flat just after ten o'clock and as the doctor stopped the car outside the tall terraced house he put his head out of the car window and looked upwards. 'There are lights on the top floor,' he announced.

'Good,' said Julia, 'that's Connie's.' She started to open the door, but he put a large gloved hand over hers and said mildly, 'Not so fast—I'll get your case. Wait there until I open the door.'

Julia did as she was told meekly, not that she was a meek girl by any means, but she had discovered in the last few days that sometimes it was nice to be told what to do. At the door she put her hand out for her case, but he shook his head. 'Lead the way up, I'll see you safely indoors.'

Connie came to the door, in her dressing gown and with her head crowned with a complexity of rollers tied into a pink hair-net. She flung her arms round Julia and exclaimed, 'Where have you been? Come in at once...' She caught sight of the doctor and asked instantly, 'Who's that?'

Julia performed the introduction with a certain amount of haste, not because she didn't want Connie to meet her companion, but because he had said that he wanted to go to his hotel as quickly as possible.

'Come in,' invited Connie, 'I'll knock up a meal and some tea,' and added as an afterthought, 'Sorry about the hair, I've just washed it.'

The doctor smiled charmingly at her, but shook his head. 'I should have liked that, but I really must go.' He turned to Julia. 'You'll have a lot to do tomorrow, I expect, so I won't bother you, but may I call for you about six? We could have a meal before we leave and iron out any problems.'

'That will do very well,' stated Julia calmly, wondering how she could bear to see him go. But he did, almost at once, and Connie closed the door and pulled her into the little sitting room and sat her down in one of the shabby armchairs by the gas fire. 'Tell me at once,' she breathed, 'where are you going?'

Julia told her while they got supper together, she told Connie about her stay in Drumlochie House too—at least, she told her most of it. It was when they were parting for the night that Connie asked, 'What about James?'

'And what about James?' asked Julia in her turn, a little coldly. 'He doesn't own me. I've never encouraged him to think that I would marry him, you know; he's conceited enough to take it for granted—and George and Maureen have egged him on...' Her beautiful black brows drew together in a frown, she looked flushed and angry and quite strikingly lovely as she stood in the doorway of Connie's spare bedroom. 'James,' she said with vehemence, 'makes me sick!'

She slept the deep sleep of the young and healthy and got up in time to cook breakfast for them both while Connie got ready to go to St Clare's. She tidied the little flat after her friend had gone, washed up and got dressed herself and went out. First to the bank for some money, then to purchase a suitable number of white uniforms and caps and a number of articles she felt it necessary to take with her. She was on her way back when her eye was caught by a wool dress with a narrow, ankle-length skirt and full sleeves caught into long tight cuffs. It had a high neck and she knew that the deep rose of its colour would suit her. She bought it recklessly and without a pang for the hole its price had made in her savings. Savings at that moment didn't matter in the least.

She had a sketchy lunch and went round to St Clare's to see Private Wing Sister, who listened to Julia's somewhat expurgated account of her journey with Miss Mary MacGall, expressed pleasure that she had got another patient so quickly and wished her luck, adding,

'So you won't be going home yet, Nurse Pennyfeather?'

Julia hedged. 'Well, not for a short time—I don't imagine that this job will last more than a week or two—probably I shall bring Miss Jason back to her home.'

She hadn't imagined anything of the sort until that moment, but it satisfied Sister, a stickler for having everything cut and dried long before it was done. 'Splendid,' she said now, 'and remember, Nurse, when you feel free to leave your sister-in-law we shall be glad to have you back with us. Matron was only saying so this morning on her round.'

Julia thanked her and got up to go; there was still George to telephone and the afternoon was advancing. She rang his office in Frome, where he had a flourishing solicitor's practice, and told him, with the brevity he always required on the telephone, what she was about to do. He wasted no words on recriminations but plunged into a reproachful speech of such tenor that if she had been listening she would have felt a complete heel; but she heard hardly a word of it; she was thinking that in two hours she would see the doctor again. When George paused for breath, she said kindly, 'I'm sure you can get a nurse from that agency in the High Street, George. I'll write from Holland. Be good. 'Bye!'

She smiled as she hung up; George hated being told to be good.

The doctor arrived punctually, but Julia was ready

and waiting for him. She was wearing her Jaeger coat and skirt of a pleasing turquoise and brown check with its matching turquoise jersey and a fur bonnet on her black hair, and had completed this outfit with brown boots and gloves and a shoulder bag. She was aware that she looked rather nice; nevertheless it was gratifying when he said quietly,

'How charming you look, Julia,' and although that was all he gave her a look of admiration which warmed a mind chilled by thoughts of Miss Marcia Jason.

They were in the car and already moving when he observed, 'It's early to dine in any of the restaurants, I thought we might go back to my hotel—there's a grill room there.'

Julia, thinking of her sandwich and cocoa lunch, felt relieved, for she was hungry. She murmured suitably and wondered which hotel it was. Something smallish, she decided, where he would be treated as a person and not a room number, because he was that sort of a man. He drove westward away from the city and presently turned into Dover Street and stopped outside Brown's Hotel.

'Is this it?' inquired Julia, a little taken aback. She didn't know much about London hotels, but she thought that this one was amongst the best of them in a quiet way. Certainly they were treated with an old-fashioned courtesy which she imagined no longer existed—probably, she reminded herself wryly, because she wasn't in the habit of frequenting such places. When they were seated the doctor said,

'I hope you're hungry—I am. I've had so much to do all day I didn't stop for a decent meal and I don't suppose you did either. Shall we have some sherry while we decide what to eat?'

They settled for Crabe à la Diable followed by baked gammon and peaches. It was while Julia was choosing a sweet that she looked up to ask apprehensively, 'Will it be rough?—the crossing, I mean. Should I not have any more?'

The doctor said on a laugh, 'I should think it will be very rough, but don't let that worry you now—I don't fancy you're the sort to be bowled over by a mere storm at sea,' and when she still looked uncertain: 'Try a water ice, that's harmless enough.'

She took his advice and as she was eating it asked, 'Are you in a hurry to be gone?'

He was sitting back in his chair, watching her. 'No,' he said slowly, 'I'm in no hurry at all—we have all the time in the world.'

Ordinary words enough, but somehow she had the impression that they had another meaning. She finished her ice, accepted his offer of coffee and sat back too.

'May I know something about my patient?' she asked in a businesslike voice.

'Your duties?' he queried smoothly. 'Would you agree to looking after her in the mornings—she needs a good deal of help still and there are exercises and so on—after lunch perhaps you would take an hour or two off, and return to duty after five o'clock until bedtime. Would a half day when it could be arranged suit you and any other reasonable time off you may wish to have? I'm sorry if it sounds a little vague, but I am a little out of touch with Marcia's progress. I'm sure no one will object to you arranging times to suit yourself.'

Very vague, Julia agreed silently, no mention of days off, and half days when they could be arranged sounded ominous; it was surprising what one did when one was in love. If he had said no off duty at all she would still have gone.

'We haven't discussed your salary,' he added, and mentioned a sum which made her raise her eyebrows. 'That's too much,' she said sharply, 'a great deal more than I could earn in England.'

'You won't be in England,' he pointed out smoothly, 'and remember you may have to alter your working hours to get up at night. My father agreed with me that it was a fair sum to offer you.'

Julia looked at him thoughtfully. 'If your father...!' she began. 'Very well, but if I don't find I have enough to do to justify all that money, I shall say so.'

He stretched a hand across the table and they solemnly shook hands. 'Done,' said the doctor, 'and there's another thing. I should much prefer you to call me Ivo—I feel distinctly elderly each time you address me so severely as Doctor.'

'All right, Ivo,' she answered, 'you still have to tell me about my patient.'

He frowned very slightly. 'I'll tell you all I know, but as I said, I haven't seen Marcia for more than six months, although I have had frequent reports and in her letters she told me that she has been making progress.' The frown deepened. 'Slow progress, I'm afraid; she should have been walking...however...!' He plunged into the details of the case and Julia, listening with eyes on his face, thought how lucky

Miss Marcia Jason was, even if she had had polio.

They started their journey soon after that and when they reached Harwich and were on board, Ivo said, 'Go to bed, Julia, it will be a rough crossing. I'll ask the stewardess to come to you presently with a bedtime drink. If you don't feel like breakfast in the morning, have something in your cabin.'

Julia, who had had ideas about staying up until the boat sailed, meekly agreed and went to her cabin. Probably Ivo didn't want her company and anyway, she was tired and her cabin, although small, seemed the height of comfort. She was undressed and in her bunk when the stewardess came in with a little tray of tea and biscuits and the strong advice to ring for her immediately she was needed. 'And I'll bring you your tea just after six, miss, and if you wish you can order breakfast then.' And when Julia thanked her and offered to pay for her tea, she was told that all that had been taken care of by the doctor. So she sipped her tea and ate a biscuit and presently, despite the uneasy movement of the boat, fell asleep. She wakened several times during the night, to feel the violent tossing of the boat and hear a multitude of creaks and groans, but she went to sleep again and only awoke when the stewardess arrived with her morning tea, and when that good lady wanted to know if she would like her breakfast in her cabin, Julia replied that no, she felt marvellous and would breakfast with the doctor and could someone tell him.

She found him waiting for her and as she sat down and wished him good morning he said, 'I hear you slept well—I'm glad, for it was a rough night. You feel like breakfast?'

'I'm hungry,' stated Julia simply, and went on to eat everything he ordered with an appetite unimpaired by the boat's sidlings. The doctor ate heartily too while they held a lively conversation upon a variety of topics until he suggested that she might like to go up on deck. The Hoek van Holland was very near now, its lights twinkling through the still dark morning, and on either side of it the dark outline of the flat coast melted away into the wild blackness. The wind was still blowing half a gale; it whipped a fine colour into her cheeks and put a sparkle into her dark eyes; she looked vividly alive and very attractive as they went below and the doctor stared at her with appreciation.

They reached Tilburg by eleven o'clock, the doctor having driven most of the way without haste. True, he had raced along the highway to Rotterdam from the Hoek, where he had been caught up in the morning traffic of that thriving city, allowing Julia time to gaze out of the window and wonder how he could ever find his way out of the maze of the crowded streets.

They ran out of the sprawling city at last, crossed a bridge over water again, and still on the *autobaan*, took the road south, past Dordrecht, over the Moeredijk bridge, towards Breda, but just as they were within sight of that city, Ivo had turned off the main road, and skirting Breda, had taken the road to Tilburg, a town, which when they reached it, Julia liked. It was surprisingly modern and looked prosperous too and was, explained Ivo as they drove through its heart, owing to its thriving woollen industry. It was also, he added, full of schools of every kind and there was a university as well.

They had left Tilburg on a quiet country road which presently ran between green fields and increasingly large clumps of trees. Now, thought Julia, it began to look more like the Holland she had imagined; even in the bare greyness of a winter's morning, the countryside had charm. But it was when Ivo turned the car into a long avenue of tall trees, their branches meeting overhead, that she exclaimed, 'Oh, this is lovely! I didn't expect it.'

The trees edged wooded land on either side, dark and still frost-covered from the night's cold, and presently she noticed that there were occasional gates barring narrow lanes leading from the road and winding away into the trees.

When she glimpsed a house, well back from the road, she asked, 'Are there people living in the woods? How quiet and peaceful it is, and how beautiful.'

Ivo looked pleased. 'You like it? My home is almost at the end of this road, close to Oisterwijk. It is quiet, but we like it like that, and even in the summer when the visitors come, we are quite undisturbed.'

He turned off the road as he spoke, through an open wooden gate and along a short sanded lane between larch trees; the lane turned abruptly and the house came into view—a pleasant house of red brick, flat-faced with big windows and a front door which looked a little too large for it. It was fair sized and Julia, looking at its solid front, thought that it might be a lot larger than it appeared. It had a neat lawn, now heavily covered with frost, and a pleasant backing of trees. As they got out of the car, the front door was opened by an elderly woman who stood back to allow a much younger woman to run out to them. She was tall and well built and Julia would have recognised her as Ivo's sister Jorina anywhere, for her features were a softer, feminine version of his and her eyes were of the same penetrating blue; only her hair, short and inclined to curl, was corn-coloured, whereas Ivo's was straight and pale. The girl ran to the car and flung herself into the doctor's arms, crying excitedly, 'Ivo—how lovely to have you home again—how I've missed you!'

She threw her arms around his neck and hugged him, then drew away a little to say to Julia, 'Forgive me—I'm so pleased to see my brother again.' Her English was fluent, but with much more of an accent than Ivo, who introduced the two girls, and waiting only long enough for them to sake hands and smile at each other, said, 'Let's get indoors—it's cold and I'm sure Julia would like to get settled in.'

They all went into the house, where Ivo paused at the door to introduce Bep, the elderly woman who had opened the door in the first place, before sweeping the two girls through the hall and into a large front room, behind whose door Julia had heard a dog barking furiously. As they entered this pleasant room a large Old English sheepdog launched himself upon the doctor, who greeted him with every sign of pleasure if slightly more calmly. 'This is Ben,' he explained, 'and you must forgive his boisterous manners, but he hasn't seen me for six months.' He fended off the dog goodnaturedly and went on, 'Let me take your coat, Julia, and do go and sit by the fire.'

Jorina said quickly, 'Yes, do, you must be cold. Bep's bringing the coffee.' She took a chair near Julia and smiled at her with friendly eyes and then turned to look at her brother when he spoke.

'I'll go up and see Marcia—is she still in the same room?'

'Yes—we wanted her to have a room downstairs now that she is at last beginning to get around a little, but she said that you would be coming home and could carry her up and down.'

She had her face turned away from Julia as she spoke and there was something in her voice which made Julia long to see her face. She looked at the doctor instead and saw an expression she couldn't make out cross his handsome features, but it had gone at once, too swiftly for her to guess at.

'Will you take Nurse Pennyfeather with you?' Jorina wanted to know, and he, without looking at Julia, said at once, 'No—time enough for that when we've had our coffee and a little talk,' and left the room.

Julia stared at the fire, telling herself that it was a relief that he hadn't wanted her to go with him, for to have had to stand by and watch their meeting after so long an absence would have been more than she could have borne. Her lively imagination was following him upstairs when it was halted by Jorina saying, 'Ivo calls you Julia, would you mind very much if I do too? And perhaps you will call me Jorina.'

She smiled again and looked so like her brother that Julia's heart bounced, but she said quietly enough, 'I'd like that very much, thank you,' and broke off as Bep came in with a big silver tray loaded with coffee cups and a plate of little sugary biscuits. She set the tray down by Jorina, lit the little spirit stove under the silver coffee pot and went away again without a word, and Jorina said as she poured the coffee,

'Old-fashioned, is it not? But my father likes it and so does Ivo, but when I marry I shall have a modern percolator which makes no work.'

'You're going to be married?' asked Julia with interest.

'Yes—in six months, perhaps sooner. My fiancé is a—how do you say—lawyer in Arnhem.'

'So your father will have to get someone to run the house?' interposed Julia, trying not to be curious but failing lamentably.

'Well, yes—to work with Bep, you know. But if Ivo marries then there may be no need, but I do not know.'

Julia bit into a biscuit because it was something to do and then had great difficulty in swallowing it, her throat was so dry. Even now Ivo was upstairs with Marcia, probably discussing the wedding date. She had been a fool to come. She closed her eyes for a brief moment, afraid that she might burst into tears, then opened them again as the door opened and Ivo came in.

He looked at her sharply as he sat down opposite her and asked,

'Do you feel all right? You look,' he hesitated, 'tired.'

Julia guessed that wasn't the word he had intended to say. She said steadily, 'Perhaps I am, but only for a minute. I think I'm excited,' and then wished she hadn't said it because she was sure that was the last thing she looked.

He must have agreed with her secret thought, for he raised an eyebrow and half smiled as he turned to Jorina. 'Marcia has progressed very well, but I'm glad I brought Julia with me, for she needs a great deal of encouragement after being an invalid for so many months.' He took the coffee cup he was offered and asked, 'How's Father?'

'Very well, but working too hard; he talks of retiring now that you are back. If you took Theo as a partner later on, you could still do your work at the hospitals and keep the practice going. Is that possible?'

'Of course—if Father will give me time to put my affairs in order first.' They began to talk about Edinburgh and the course he had been following there and became so absorbed in their talk that Julia was surprised to hear the lovely old painted clock on the wall strike twelve, and so it seemed was Ivo, for he paused in what he was saying and exclaimed, 'Julia, how thoughtless I am—you shall go to your room and then I'll take you to meet Marcia.'

Julia followed Jorina upstairs, stifling the idea that the last thing she wanted to do was to see Marcia. She would be with her for most of the day from now on and might not see Ivo at all, and even if she did, never alone. She sighed inwardly and crossed the landing behind Jorina and into a long passage leading to the back of the house. She had been right; the house had a sizeable wing behind as well as a floor

above the one they were now on Jorina opened the
first door they came to.

'Marcia's room is in the front of the house—' she
waved an arm vaguely. 'We've had a bell fixed so
that if she should want you she can ring, but she's so
good I don't expect she will ever use it.'

Julia heard faint mockery behind the words and
wondered about it, then forgot it in the pleasure of
seeing her room. It was furnished most elegantly and
with great comfort in the Adam period, with curtains
and bedspread of pink striped silk, a pale echo of the
deeper pink of the carpeted floor. There was a small
buttonbacked chair too with a small table beside it
and a writing desk in the window. There were even
books piled on a dainty little wall table. Jorina asked,
'You like it? The bathroom is across the passage and
is for you alone. Now I leave you and presently Ivo
will come.' She went to the door. 'I am glad that you
are here,' she said with a sincerity which was heart-
warming.

Left to herself, Julia spent a few minutes exploring
her room. It was indeed comfortable, almost luxuri-
ous. She unpacked a few things and went to find the
bathroom—pale pink to match the bedroom and furnished with an abundance of towels and soaps and
bath salts. Julia heaved a sigh of pleasure at the sight
of them. Even if she was going to be lonely here, it
would all be most comfortable.

She had tidied herself and was standing by the window looking out upon the wintry scene outside when
Ivo knocked and came in. He said rather shortly
'Ready?' and stood aside as she went through the
door, then led her across the landing where he opened

a beautifully carved door and said, 'Come in, won't you?'

The room was beautiful, with a high ceiling like the sitting room and just as beautifully decorated with plaster work. The walls were hung with striped silk in a very pale blue and there was a fire burning in the steel grate and a great many pictures about the walls. The bed was a little ornate for Julia's taste; she didn't like French furniture herself, although she had to admit that it was beautiful enough. There were several easy chairs and a daybed upon which her patient was lying. Julia walked across to it and stood looking down at its occupant while the doctor introduced her. As she shook the languid hand held out to her she took stock of Miss Marcia Jason and instantly disliked what she saw. Miss Jason was a pale blonde with a long face, rendered thin by illness, no doubt, but possessing a kind of beaky, austere beauty which Julia found distinctly chilling. She had pale blue eyes framed in long colourless lashes and a mouth that was too thin and which was now turned down at its corners in a sweetly sad way which made Julia quite out of patience. It was impossible to see how tall Miss Jason was as she was lying down, but all that was visible of her looked ethereal, even if flat-chested. She said now in a sweetly gracious voice, 'Dear Ivo, to bring me my very own nurse. I know you'll help me to bear my burdens—I've done my best, but sometimes I have felt that I needed someone—robust upon whom to lean.'

Julia said 'Oh, yes?' politely. No one had ever called her robust before. She became aware that her junoesque curves might strike someone of Marcia's meagre proportions in that light, and probably the doctor, loving the tiresome creature before her, shared her views. Julia blushed at the thought and blushed anew when her patient said, 'There—have I been too outspoken? I've always considered that the truth is all-important, but I have no wish to offend you.'

Julia managed to smile quite nicely. 'I'm not offended,' she said serenely. 'I hope that before I go, I shall be able to give you some of my robustness so that you can get out and about and enjoy life again.'

'But I enjoy myself now—I've forced myself to bow to circumstance and I'm aware that I shall never be as others are. All the same—' she cast what Julia could only describe as a melting look at the doctor, 'I still have a number of attributes, I believe, and am not altogether wanting in intellect. Ivo will tell you of our conversations when we first met and of the letters I've written. I'm a good letter writer.'

Julia said a trifle woodenly, 'That's an accomplishment these days.' She had never before met anyone so conceited and self-complacent; moreover, she suspected that Miss Jason, in other circumstances, would have been on her feet by now and struggling back to a normal way of living. She had a tussle ahead of her, and for what? she asked herself bitterly: so that this pale creature should become the doctor's wife? She said bracingly,

'I'll come back after lunch and we can talk a little and perhaps you will tell me how far you've progressed, then we can work out a routine.'

Miss Jason gave a silvery laugh. 'Routine? My dear nurse, I have no routine—how is that possible with my state of health? You find it difficult, a jolly, buxom girl like yourself, to understand how we frailer women feel. But we'll have our little talk by all means, for I'm sure you mean it for the best.'

She smiled, the same sweet smile, and Julia smiled back over gritted teeth. It had been bad enough to be called robust; now she was jolly and—unforgivable— buxom. The girl was detestable!

She went out of the room without looking at the doctor. He seemed like a stranger now; not the resourceful friendly man she had spent those days at Drumlochie House with, or the calm man telling her what to do at the accident on the M1 and then holding her close while she cried. This man beside her was calm, but withdrawn too, as though everything they had done together had been forgotten. Perhaps it had.

She went downstairs beside him without speaking and sat soberly throughout lunch, which they ate in a small bright room at the back of the house. The conversation, sustained easily enough by Ivo and his sister, was lively enough and covered a whole range of subjects, but Miss Jason wasn't mentioned once.

It was after they had left the dining room that Ivo asked her to go with him to his study—a large room, Julia discovered, lined with books and surprisingly tidy. He waved her to a chair and sat down at his desk.

'Marcia has made great progress,' he began, 'though I had hoped that she would have been more active, but you can see that she needs encouragement—she has the idea that she will never be quite well again, which indeed she will be if only she will make the effort.' He gave Julia a fierce, daunted look and went on harshly, 'I have a great regard for her, Julia, I hope that you will help her.'

Julia nodded, wondering why it was he found it necessary to remind her so frequently that he had a great regard for Marcia. Once was enough—too much, she thought. 'Of course I will,' she said cheerfully. 'I'll start slowly, don't worry, but I'll persist. Can I have precise instructions?'

'You will have to ask my father for those. Marcia is not of course my patient. I do know that she is capable of walking with support. She needs other interests.'

'Well, she's got them now you're back.' Julia's voice was very even. She got up and walked to the door. 'I'll get into uniform and go to her now,' and Ivo who had gone to the door with her said suddenly, 'Julia, it's impossible...' She gave him a kind smile, for of course he was worrying about his Marcia. 'No, Ivo, it's not—nothing's impossible if you set your heart on it!' She walked past him and crossed the hall and went slowly up the stairs, her lovely head held high.

CHAPTER FOUR

THE ELDER Doctor van den Werff came home after tea. Julia was in her room unpacking and when Bep knocked on the door and signed to her to go downstairs, she did so. She had changed into her new white uniform and made up a muslin cap, and so attired went quickly down to the hall, rather uncertain as to where she was to go. She need not have worried, for Ivo was waiting for her. He said at once,

'I hope we don't disturb you, but my father is anxious to meet you and evening surgery is in half an hour. His study is over here.'

He led the way across the hall and opened a door on the opposite side to the sitting room and motioned her inside. The man who stood waiting for her was as tall as his son and just as big. His hair, not yet wholly grey, receded from the same wide forehead, his eyes were just as blue and his mouth just as kind. Julia, who had been rather dreading this moment, smiled radiantly at him, for after all, he was only Ivo in thirty years' time and therefore no stranger. She said, 'How do you do, doctor,' in a quiet voice and took the seat he offered her as he took his own chair behind his desk. Ivo, who had followed her in, perched on its side, one long leg swinging. Julia looked around her; the room was obviously used as a consulting room as well as a study—there was a couch along one wall and a glass case with instru-

ments tidily arranged inside it and a hand basin on
one corner, half hidden by a screen. She finished her
survey and turned her gaze on the older man, who
smiled in his turn.

'We're very glad indeed to have you with us, Miss
Pennyfeather,' he began. 'I hope that you will be
happy while you are here—I assure you we shall do
our best to make you so.' He shifted his chair a little
so that he could get a better view of her face and
went on, 'And what do you think of your patient?'

Julia hesitated. It really wouldn't do to tell him her
opinion of Miss Jason; she might get sent back to
England by the next train if she did. She had spent a
couple of hours with Marcia during the afternoon and
had to admit to herself that her hastily formed opinion
hadn't been changed in the least. It had, if anything,
become firmer. She had, after a polite, exhausting ar-
gument, got her patient to her feet and walked her a
few steps about the room, an act which had served to
strengthen her suspicion that her companion could do
a good deal more than she would have everyone else
suppose. Julia, remembering her promise to Ivo, encouraged her gently and assured her that within a very
short time she would find herself walking normally—
even going downstairs. They would start tomorrow,
said Julia in her kind, firm voice, but this evening
Doctor van den Werff had said that he would carry
Miss Jason down to a family dinner party.

She had left the room, the memory of the smug
little smile on her patient's face very vivid in her
memory. She said now, weighing her words, 'Miss
Jason seems to have reached a period of inactivity,
but that often happens, doesn't it? I think that now

Ivo has returned it will give her the encouragement she needs to make the final effort to return to a normal life. It must be difficult after months of doing nothing much. How many months is it?'

'Ten. You're right, nurse, and I applaud my son's happy idea of bringing you back with him. This is a fairly quiet household; perhaps Marcia has been too much on her own.'

Julia pinkened. 'I didn't mean that,' she protested. 'I sound as though I'm criticising my patient. I'm not, but I promised Ivo that I would get her well and I will, only I think I should tell you what I think.'

She paused after this speech, drew breath, and sat silently waiting for someone to say something. It was Ivo who broke the silence, and he spoke in a silky voice she had never heard before. 'And are you sure that you are not overestimating your powers, Julia? I am aware that you are a capable and efficient nurse, but surely not such a very experienced one?'

Julia's bosom heaved as she got to her feet and stood facing him, her head very erect, her eyes flashing. 'If you feel,' she said in austere tones, 'that you've made a mistake in bringing me here, I'll pack my things and go back on the next train.'

Ivo had risen too, and they stared at each other for a long a moment until he said, 'Julia, I beg your pardon—I'm behaving like a pompous ass and I don't mean a word of it—put it down to worry if you will. The last thing I want you to do is to go away.'

Julia's heart somersaulted under her white uniform. She said with admirable calm, 'Then I won't,' and sat down again, and Ivo's father, who had sat silently watching them, gave a dry little cough and remarked,

'Very well, now that the air is cleared, shall we put our heads together?' He smiled at Julia, 'And may I call you Julia, young lady? My son appears to do so and I can see no reason why I should not if you have no objection.'

Julia beamed at him. 'I'd like you to,' she said, and he nodded and went on, 'Now I will tell you all I can about Marcia, for we are as anxious as you are to get her fit again. She was in Holland on a short study tour—probably Ivo has already told you that she is a highly qualified teacher of marked intelligence. She and Ivo met at a reception in Tilburg,' he paused and looked at Julia from hooded eyes. 'They had much in common and she visited us frequently. It wasn't until the day she came to say goodbye and arrange to see Ivo in England that she became ill. She had been feeling poorly for a day or two—headache, sore throat— you know all the symptoms, of course—she was actually with us when the paralysis set in. She was in hospital for three months and then returned here where she has been ever since. She—er—bore her illness with almost saintlike fortitude and when she asked if she might come here until she was strong enough to travel home, we were only too glad to offer her hospitality. As I am sure you have gathered from Ivo, he and Marcia...' He left the sentence in the air for Julia to finish as she thought best and went 'Marcia's serious mind is a great attraction to him, you understand.'

He sat back and looked at Julia and she looked back at him and could have sworn that behind those half closed lids, his eyes were alight with laughter.

She asked herself silently why and commented soberly,

'A terrible thing to happen...'

'Yes. Now as to her drugs and treatment—' He became all at once professional and remained so until Julia finally rose to her feet when he got up too, saying, 'I hope you will come to me with any difficulty however small, Julia, and if I am not here, Ivo will be, I daresay. I shall see you at dinner and I look forward to that.'

Julia went back to her patient and helped her change into a dark red velvet dress which drained all the colour from her already pale face and was cut far too tight. Julia, zipping it up the back, remarked cheerfully that the dress was a little close-fitting—a good sign because it meant that her patient was putting on weight, whereupon Miss Jason replied indignantly that she had put on too much weight over the past months and was anxious to lose a few pounds. 'For,' she said with what Julia chose to call a simper, 'we slim girls owe it to ourselves to keep our figures, don't you agree?' She gave her high clear laugh. 'Though of course, Nurse Pennyfeather, I expect you find that a piece of nonsense.' She added, 'Do you never diet?'

'Never,' said Julia goodnaturedly.

'Should you not?' persisted Miss Jason. 'You are a little—if you'll forgive me—plump, are you not?'

Julia refused to get annoyed. 'I feel like Juno,' she said with a chuckle. 'Thank you for the compliment.' Which silenced Miss Jason most effectively.

They dined in a small panelled room behind the doctor's study, the five of them sitting round an oval

Empire table covered with a fine white linen cloth and set with heavy silver and a quantity of cut glass. After dinner Marcia begged, with a great deal of unnecessary charm, to be allowed to stay up, managing to imply at the same time that she was a little afraid of what Julia might say if she did. Julia, listening to her and feeling like a tyrant, asked, 'Did I really order you to bed after dinner? I don't remember doing so— I must have been out of my mind if I did. Why on earth shouldn't you stay up until a reasonable hour if you wish? There's no reason why you shouldn't.' And had the satisfaction of seeing her patient frown and disclaim any pretensions to enough strength to remain up late.

Half an hour later Doctor van den Werff was called out to a case, but before he could get to his feet, Ivo was already at the door.

'Let me, Vader,' he said decisively. 'You've had a long day—I know the Bakker children well enough, and I daresay it's nothing serious; you know how nervous Mevrouw Bakker is.' He looked round the room, saying, 'You'll all forgive me, I know.'

He stared at Julia and then past her to Marcia who was speaking in a tiresomely reasonable voice which somehow conveyed that her feelings were hurt. 'Your first night back,' she said gently, 'and I had so much to tell you about my studies of Vondel's work—your father was kind enough to get me the English translation...'

Ivo interrupted her gently and with carefully hidden irritation.

'I'm sorry, Marcia, there will be time later on for

us to talk. I'm home for good, you know. I'll see you in the morning.'

He was almost through the door when Marcia said plaintively, 'I'm sure I don't know who is to get me upstairs. Must I spend the night here?'

Her words fell upon her companions' ears, but not upon Ivo's, for he had gone. Before anyone else could speak, Julia said briskly,

'Just the opportunity we need, Miss Jason—imagine what a triumph for you when you tell Ivo that you went upstairs on your own two legs!'

Her patient gave her a fixed look. 'Why do you call Doctor van den Werff Ivo?' she wanted to know.

'He asked me to. You see, when we were at Drumlochie House it was rather—rather like make-believe, if you know what I mean, and it would have been ridiculous if we had been formal with each other. I expect you've heard him call me Julia, haven't you?' She smiled at Marcia's cross face. 'I expect you would have done the same in those circumstances.'

'I doubt it. I hope you don't expect me to call you Julia. I shall address you as Nurse. Is that not correct?'

'Quite,' said Julia dryly. She turned to Doctor van den Werff, who had been sitting quietly listening to every word.

'What do you think, doctor?' she asked. 'May I help Miss Jason to her room? We have a stick here and the stairs are shallow and the balustrade strong. It would be a marvellous surprise for Ivo, wouldn't it?'

'Indeed, yes, Julia. Do so by all means.' He turned to Marcia. 'My dear,' he said mildly, 'think how pleased he is going to be—your first positive step to a normal life.' His voice was serious, but Julia felt sure that if only she could have seen his eyes, they would have been twinkling at some joke of his own.

There was a great deal of fuss getting Marcia on to her feet, for she didn't want to, which made it twice as hard. But eventually Julia, by sheer stubbornness, had her standing, and after more fuss, walking slowly, leaning heavily on Julia's arm and wielding the stick with unnecessary clumsiness. Going upstairs was a lengthy business, punctuated by Marcia's dignified protests and audible sighs; she even so far forgot herself at one point to observe that Julia was a hard young woman, devoid of all sympathy, to which Julia replied,

'Yes, I'm sure I must seem so to you, and I do sympathise, but I want to help you to get quite well, you know, and once you've done this, you'll find it will get easier and easier. Sit on the stairs a minute and get your second wind.'

Thus cheerfully admonished, Miss Jason allowed herself to be gently lowered on to the staircase and Julia sat down beside her, 'For,' she said in her friendly voice, 'we might as well be comfortable.'

'Comfortable?' echoed Marcia bitterly. 'I shall never…' She broke off as Jorina and her father came out of the sitting room to gaze up at them from the hall.

'I knew you could do it if you tried, Marcia,' said the doctor. 'I can see you'll soon be getting around like the rest of us.'

Marcia allowed her long face to break into a wistful smile.

'You have no idea of the struggle I've had, Doctor van den Werff, but I will not give in—I should have been in my room by now if Nurse hadn't commanded me to take a rest—though I own I'm quite exhausted.'

Julia saw the faint frown on the doctor's face. 'You must not do too much,' he began. 'Nurse, perhaps we had better carry Miss Jason to her room.'

Julia presented him with an untroubled face, although her thoughts were the reverse. She was as certain as she could be that Marcia was far stronger in the legs than she would have them believe. But she had, after all, only just arrived and the fact that she disliked her patient could be influencing her judgement, though she felt that unlikely; she was too well trained for that. She said now, 'If Ivo isn't going to be too long, shall we stay here? Then he can see for himself how well she has managed and carry her the rest of the way.'

The doctor was about to debate this when the front door opened and Ivo joined them. He began. 'Hello, Vader, a false alarm—the baby...' and then he stopped and stared up the staircase to where Marcia and Julia, looking a very ill-assorted pair, were sitting.

'What on earth are you doing?' he demanded. 'Marcia, don't tell me you got there on your own legs?'

Julia had known that Marcia would take full advantage of the situation, and she proceeded to do so now. 'Are you surprised, Ivo? Nurse insisted that I walked upstairs to my room, and I've been absolutely terrified, but I've managed to get as far as this, and now you're back and I'll go on again so that you can see for yourself, though I confess I'm ready to drop.'

She gave a trill of laughter, a combination of courage and weariness and gentle resignation to the great bully of a nurse beside her. 'Isn't it lucky that Nurse is such a strong girl? If I'm to be forced to walk everywhere, she will need to pick me up a dozen times a day.'

He was halfway up the stairs. 'What a wonderful surprise for my first day home,' he said lightly, and bent and lifted her and carried her into her room, put her gently on the bed, said goodnight equally gently and went away, standing aside for Julia as she followed them, without looking at her. Only as he turned to go did he catch her eye and she knew that he was holding his anger in check. Later on, she judged, she would be told off.

But first there was Miss Jason to get to bed—a slow business because she had known that Julia had been shown in a bad light and she wanted to extract as much pleasure from the fact as possible by making sly references to the episode whenever she could turn the conversation to her liking. But Julia parried her oblique remarks easily enough, talking about anything which came into her head and refusing to rise to any of her patient's barbed remarks. At length she said goodnight and went downstairs again; if there was going to be a row, she might just as well get it over.

Apparently Ivo felt the same way, for he opened his study door as she reached the foot of the stairs and requested her in a quiet voice to join him. He bade her sit down, still very quiet, and asked in a beautifully controlled rage, 'And what in the name of thunder have you been doing?'

Julia, during the slow half hour of putting Marcia to bed, had had time to think. She said reasonably, 'It seemed to be a good idea to start Miss Jason off in the way she must go. She has to make the effort, you know—what better moment to start, with the incentive of your delighted surprise when you returned?'

He said, in low-voiced fury, 'I can conceive of nothing less likely to give me delight—Marcia is a very delicate woman.'

'Fiddlesticks,' said Julia, who hadn't meant to say that at all but hadn't been able to restrain herself. 'Miss Jason has been very ill; she's better, admit it. If you were checking a patient in hospital in as good a physical condition as hers, wouldn't you prescribe as much exercise as she could manage within reason? She should have been doing far more than she is.'

He came and stood over her. 'Aren't you presuming a little too much, nurse?' His voice was dangerous. 'And how could you know what I would prescribe for my patients?'

'Oh, I don't,' said Julia, 'I only guessed,' and he made an exasperated sound which she ignored. 'I'm trying to help you and Miss Jason—I said I would, if you remember.' She went on in a reasonable voice, 'But if you want her to stay bedbound, please tell me and I'll nurse her exactly as you wish—blanket baths, meals in bed, pressure points—the lot.'

She drew breath after this outrageous speech and looked at him to see what he would say. He looked so forbidding that she let it out very slowly so that he shouldn't see that she was just a little frightened of him. He said through clenched teeth, 'You take too much upon yourself, Miss Pennyfeather. I should very much like to…' He closed his lips and to her regret, didn't finish the sentence.

She said, her dark eyes very bright, 'I seem to remember you saying not a couple of hours since that you didn't wish me to go. And,' she added for good measure, 'do you have to be quite so bad-tempered?'

He was suddenly bland, his fine rage nicely under control. 'Don't tell me, my dear girl, that anything I should say or do could affect your actions in any way. It is unfortunate that you move me to anger rather more than most people.'

'You're quite right,' said Julia disconcertingly. 'You were angry with me the first time we met because I opened that door.' She added indignantly, 'And if I hadn't you'd still be standing there, frozen to death!'

To her surprise he gave a shout of laughter. 'Julia, you're impossible! I began by being furious with you and now...' He caught her round the waist and when she looked up at him, kissed her quite roughly on the mouth. Julia made no attempt to free herself from his arms, but stood stiffly within them, her eyes on his shirt front. She said quietly while her heart rocked under her neat uniform,

'I quite understand that you're happy to be home again doctor, but wouldn't it be better if you kissed the right girl?'

He showed no sign of penitence and made no effort to loosen his hold, but said idly, 'What a little waist you have. And who is the right girl?'

She gave him an open-mouthed look. 'Why, Miss Jason, of course. She was telling me about—about you this afternoon.' She took a deep breath and went on, 'I'm sorry that I annoy you so much—I'll keep out of your way as much as I can.'

He ignored this. 'What did Marcia have to say?' he asked in a mild voice which lulled her into answering, 'That you were a brilliantly clever man with a great future and that you needed a—a helpmate with a similar brain and that she was glad to have at last found a man who disliked levity unless it was relevant to the occasion and...'

He asked with interest, 'Are you making all this up?'

'No—I wouldn't know how to. But it must be nice for you, and for her, of course.' She gently disengaged his arms from about her person and he dropped them to his side and took a step or so away from her.

When he spoke his voice was quiet. 'There's no need to keep out of my way. Even when you annoy me I enjoy your company.' His eyes searched her face. 'I must explain if I can—at Drumlochie it was as if we lived in another world—it seemed more real than this one. I forgot for the time the obligations which I had. They didn't seem to matter—when you opened the door, you opened it on to make believe, although I'm not sure now if it wasn't real.' He stopped. 'I'm not explaining very well.'

'No,' agreed Julia in a wooden voice, 'you're not, but I understand very well what you mean. You forgot all about Miss Jason waiting for you. It's a pity you didn't remember—you might not have asked me to come back with you.'

It surprised her when he smiled. 'No, I think it will turn out to be a very good thing that you came. You'll get Marcia fit.'

Julia walked over to the stove and held out her hands to its warmth.

'Will you marry her when she's well?' she asked coolly.

Her voice had been cool, his was suddenly icy. 'That, Miss Pennyfeather, is entirely my own business.'

There was a little devil inside Julia, egging her on. She walked to the door. 'Well, of course it is, but I like to know how much time I have—can you wait until she's absolutely fit or are you so eager to marry her that you'll be content with a semi-invalid?'

He covered the room in a couple of strides and took her by the shoulders, shook her until the teeth rattled in her head and then let her go and stood staring at her with a set face. She stared back, appalled at what she had said. At length she spoke from a throat gone dry. 'That was dreadful of me—I'm sorry, I didn't mean a word of it. I don't know why...please forgive me.'

She left him abruptly and went up to her room, to sit on her bed going over and over the scene in his study and wondering what had possessed her to behave so badly. Presently she undressed, had a bath and then, ready for bed, went along to see if there was anything more she could do for Miss Jason.

'Nothing, thank you,' stated Miss Jason firmly. 'I'm relaxed both in mind and body, despite your rough treatment of the latter, Nurse,' this with a little laugh to indicate that she was joking. 'I shan't need you until the morning. Good-night.'

Julia, still meek, went back to her own room and got into bed, where she lay warm and comfortable, reading the same page of a book she had picked up from the table, and wishing with all her heart that she was back at Drumlochie House, huddled in bed in her ice-cold bedroom, knowing that just down the corridor Ivo was stretched out on his fourposter ready to come at once if she should want him—not the Ivo she had been talking to an hour ago, but the Ivo she had first met in that other, happier world.

She saw only Jorina and Bep when she went downstairs in the morning. Marcia was still asleep; it seemed a good idea to have breakfast before she wakened. Jorina greeted her warmly, inquired as to whether she had slept well and been warm enough and went on:

'Father and I thought you would be down again later in the evening, but Ivo said he had had a talk with you and you had gone to bed. I expect you were tired.' She gave Julia a smiling glance. 'Or was Ivo cross about something? I thought I heard his voice…something's worrying, though I don't know what, he'd only been in the house for ten minutes for me to see that. Have some more coffee? I hope you don't find our breakfasts too strange after your eggs and bacon.' She handed Julia her cup and passed her a dish of cheese. 'Try some of this on your bread, it tastes good. Are you going to get Marcia down today?'

Julia was soothed by Jorina's pleasant acceptance of her company. She said readily, 'Yes, going down will be much easier. Is—will Ivo be in to lunch? If not, I'll wait until the afternoon and Miss Jason can be down waiting for him and he can help her in the evening—that should encourage her.'

'I'm sure it will.' Jorina's voice was dry. 'He won't be back until about five—he's in Tilburg today, but hc'll be helping with the surgery this evening. If you bring her down about three o'clock we could have a cup of tea together. When are you to be free?'

Julia gave her a grateful look. No one had mentioned off duty and she had forgotten to ask about it; anyway, the opportunity hadn't presented itself. 'I don't know. Ivo said something about one or two half days each week and a day off when it could be arranged. He didn't say anything definite about off duty.'

'Well, how about this afternoon? If you bring Marcia downstairs about three and go off until six?' She slipped an arm into Julia's. 'I hope you will be happy with us—it will be nice to have someone to talk to. There's Marcia, of course,' she added hastily, 'but I'm not clever, you see, and I bore her.'

It was an hour later, while Julia was supervising Marcia's exercises, that a visitor was announced to see that young lady.

'Mijnheer August de Winter,' said Bep stolidly from the door, and Julia was surprised to see the delight in Marcia's long face—much more delight than she had shown towards Ivo, for all her gentle speeches to him. Julia, on her way to the door with a murmured, 'I'll leave you,' was stopped long enough to be introduced as 'my nurse Ivo brought back with him in the hope of getting me strong again,' and then Marcia turned her pale eyes on her and explained, 'This is Mijnheer de Winter, a schoolmaster in Tilburg, who has been good enough to keep me company whenever he has had the time to spare.'

Julia watched her patient simper—really, the woman was fifty years behind the times! She be-

longed in a Victorian novel. She didn't think much
of Mijnheer de Winter either; his face was even
longer than Marcia's and his eyes pale. He had mousy
hair, brushed neatly across the baldness on top of his
head, and a mean little mouth. Julia went out of the
room, closing the door softly behind her, thinking that
the pair of them were exactly right for each other.
Hard on that thought came another. Did Ivo know
about her patient's visitor?

She went along to her room and wrote a letter, and
when she went back after a little while with her patient's lunch tray, it was to find her alone once more.

Marcia held up a massive tome for her to see and
cried in her wispy voice, 'You see, nurse, how kind
Mijnheer de Winter is. He came especially to bring
me this volume of Virgil—I happened to mention that
I should like to read it once more.' She smiled and
said almost playfully, 'Don't mention his visit to Doctor van den Werff—I mean Ivo, of course, I don't
want to make him jealous and I've not had the time
to tell him about August's visits yet.'

Julia lifted the lid off the omelette she had borne
upstairs. 'I don't tell tales,' she remarked briefly. 'I
hope you enjoy your lunch.'

She didn't enjoy her own, although she pretended
to for Jorina's sake. The more she saw of her patient
the less she liked her. She was reasonably sure that
Marcia had the full use of her arms and legs and for
some reason didn't want anyone to know, not for the
moment—and now she was sly as well. And there
was really nothing that Julia could do about it.

After several false starts and a great deal of shil-
lyshallying on the stairs, Marcia got down them rather

well, probably, thought Julia nastily, because there was no one to see except herself. It was already past three o'clock, for her patient, although she knew that Julia was to be free at that hour, had contrived a number of last-minute hindrances. Julia drank a hasty cup of tea and went to change out of her uniform. A quarter of an hour later she was walking down the road, thinking to herself that if she disliked her patient, the feeling was reciprocated, although she doubted if either of them would admit it. It was already dusk, for it had been a dull cold day, with grey cloud overhead and a blustery wind—it would be dark by the time she had walked the mile or so into Oisterwijk, but it was a main road and she couldn't very well miss her way back.

By the time she had looked round the little town it was five o'clock and almost dark, so she headed for home again. She had walked for ten minutes or more when she discovered that she was on the wrong road. She retraced her steps, found the right way, and started off once more.

A car raced past her towards the town, its lights blazing so that when it had gone by the dark seemed even darker; she heard its brakes squeal as it stopped and turned and came back towards her, its powerful headlamps pinpointing her in the night. She didn't change her pace, nor did she look round. Even when the car dropped to a crawl beside her she looked steadily ahead. It went past her and drew up and Ivo's voice, very quiet, said, 'Get in, Julia.'

She did as she was told, not in the least deceived by his tone. As she slid into the seat beside him, she could almost feel his anger. But she wasn't going to allow herself to be intimidated. 'How nice,' she said chattily as he leaned over her to shut the door. 'Are you on your way home?'

'I've been home.' He started the car, driving slowly, and her heart began to hammer because she was so very conscious of him close beside her. She edged away carefully to stop rigid as he said, still quiet,

'You don't need to do that. I'm not going to hit you, tough heaven knows—what possessed you to go out in the dark?'

She could hear by his voice that he was still holding back rage and made haste to say in mollifying tones, 'Well, there wasn't time during the day and I wanted to go for a walk and I thought it would be nice to see Oisterwijk. It's pretty, isn't it? and the shops are nice, only I couldn't buy anything.'

He made a sound which might have been a laugh. 'Why not? Don't tell me you allowed the language to stand in your way.'

'No, I don't think I would have done, but I had no money—Dutch money.'

He turned the car into the short lane leading to the house and stopped and turned to peer at her through the dark. He said evenly,

'You shall have money tomorrow. I'm sorry about that, I should have thought of it.'

Julia stirred, a little uneasy; he was being so very calm. She was mistaken, for when next he spoke his voice was very nearly a snarl.

'Don't dare to do this again, Julia. What a little fool you are—good God, anything might have happened to you! Supposing you had been given a lift...!'

She interrupted him a little indignantly, 'Two cars stopped, but I didn't go with them because I wasn't quite sure where the house was in the dark and it might have been difficult to make the driver understand.'

'You are not to accept lifts...!'

'But I just have,' she pointed out calmly, 'from you.'

She heard his sharp indrawn breath. 'Don't be frivolous,' he said violently. 'I came to look for you.'

Her heart bounced against her ribs, but her voice was still coolly calm. 'I didn't know—thank you. I hope I haven't spoiled your evening.' She thought him most unreasonable when he answered abruptly, 'You might have thought of that sooner.'

Julia protested, 'How could I? I wasn't to know that you would come and look for me. I think you're being unreasonable, and I'm twenty-two, you know, and quite capable of looking after myself. Thank you all the same,' she added politely.

She heard him sigh. 'Perhaps you will be good enough to go walking in daylight—and if you must go to Oisterwijk, or anywhere else, after dark, please ask one of us to run you there in a car.' His hand came down on hers, linked in her lap. 'Please, Julia.'

She wanted to take his hand in hers. It was an effort to keep her hands resting quietly under his touch. She said at once, 'Yes, of course I'll do what you ask. I hope you're not—not angry any more.'

His hand tightened for a moment and slid away. He said in a very quiet voice, 'Oh, my dear girl,' and then in a normal voice, 'Have you had a busy day with Marcia? I hear she walked downstairs.'

Julia gave him a cheerful account of the day's doings, omitting the small frictions between herself and her patient. They were unimportant; the important thing was to get Marcia well so that this man beside her could marry her, since he wanted to. She sighed soundlessly.

After dinner Doctor van den Werff declared that he had letters to write and within a few minutes Jorina got up too, saying that she was going to telephone Klaas, which left Marcia lying gracefully on one of the sofas by the fire, Ivo sitting opposite her in a great armchair with Ben at his feet, listening with apparent interest to her opinion of Goethe's works, and Julia, sitting a little apart.

When Marcia paused for breath Julia got to her feet with the fictitious statement that she had letters to write. 'And I'll get your room ready for you, Miss Jason, and come back presently, and we'll try walking upstairs. Shall we say two hours?'

Ivo raised his eyes briefly from the contemplation of his well-shod feet. 'If you intend walking upstairs, Marcia, I shouldn't make it too late—it would never do to overdo things.' He glanced at Julia. 'Would you come back in an hour, Julia?' His voice held mild authority and although Marcia pouted prettily, he took no notice. As Julia went from the room she heard him ask,

'And what do you think of Vondel—not much known...'

She had expected her patient to make a great fuss about going upstairs, but as she reached their foot,

leaning on Ivo's arm, Doctor van den Werff flung
open his study door to say that Ivo was wanted on
the telephone at once, and without him for an audience there was no point in drooping and sighing. Julia
got her to bed, said goodnight and went along to her
room; she might as well go to bed too. She had taken
off her cap when Jorina appeared. 'I've made some
coffee,' she said persuasively, 'come on down and
have a cup.'

They went together to the empty sitting room and
over their coffee talked about Jorina's wedding. They
were deep in the bridesmaids' outfits when the two
men came in and their chat became the pleasant end-
of-day talk Julia remembered so clearly at Drumlochie House. And when after a little while she got up
to go to bed it was Ivo who said,

'Not yet, Julia, unless you're very tired.' He put
down his coffee cup. 'Jorina, I haven't had time to
tell you about the delicious bread Julia baked...'

It was when she at length got up to go that Ivo said
at the door,

'There's something I want to know. Why do you
call Marcia Miss Jason?'

'She prefers it—some patients do, you know, just
as they prefer to call the nurse by her full name. It
doesn't mean anything.' She looked anxiously at him.
'We get on famously,' she lied, and smiled, 'She's
been simply wonderful today.'

'Has she? It must have been very lonely for her all
these months—she has no friends here and no visitors, only Jorina and her girl friends, and they...
You'll be good company for her. She told me this
evening how very empty her days have been.'

Julia nodded, said goodnight and went upstairs. So Marcia hadn't told him about Mijnheer de Winter after all.

CHAPTER FIVE

A WEEK WENT BY, one day slipping without haste into the next, and Marcia, whether she liked it or not, showed marked improvement. Julia had managed to get some sort of routine into the days, and now her patient was coming down before lunch instead of after—something she didn't seem to like very much, and it wasn't until Mijnheer de Winter called again and Marcia was forced to entertain him in the sitting room with Jorina and Julia there that Julia realised why—her patient's caller had looked decidedly taken aback when he had been shown in and had stayed, making rather self-conscious conversation, for a bare ten minutes.

Later that day, when Julia had been alone with Jorina, she had asked about him and Jorina had laughed and said, 'Oh, him. Isn't he a pompous little man? Marcia told me that Ivo finds him agreeable, though, and is grateful to him for visiting her all the while he's been in Scotland. All I can say is that Ivo must have changed a great deal if he likes him.' She eyed Julia, placidly making up a muslin cap, with a thoughtful look. 'He has changed.'

Julia didn't look up. 'Well,' she said reasonably, 'he does bring her the kind of book she enjoys.'

'Homer, Virgil,' said Jorina with something like disgust. 'I'd rather browse through *Elle*.' She put down the sweater she was knitting. 'Julia, do you think she's a bit too clever?'

Julia clasped her hands round her knees and thought. Determined to be quite fair, she said at length, 'It depends on whom she marries, doesn't it? I expect some men admire a good brain—if they're clever themselves.'

'Well, Klaas is clever, and I don't know one end of the Greek alphabet from the other,' Jorina smiled, 'but he admires me.'

It was when the question of Julia's half days came up that Marcia suggested that Jorina should take her into Tilburg one afternoon.

'I'm quite able to amuse myself for an hour or so,' she said with her habitual gravity, and smiled bravely when, Ivo said,

'That's very kind of you, Marcia, but will you be quite all right on your own?' Whereupon she had leaned forward and pressed his hand and murmured, 'You forget, Ivo, that I've had many months alone and in pain.'

Julia squirmed in embarrassment and looked away so as not to see Ivo's face, and met his father's stare instead. She saw the gleam of laughter in his eyes before he allowed their lids to fall.

So she had gone to Tilburg with Jorina and enjoyed it immensely, for she had some money now and a pleasant companion with whom to look at the shops. She bought presents for her family, because no one had said how long she was going to stay and for all she knew she might not have the chance of shopping again. They went back after tea when the pale winter sky had darkened and the wind had gathered its strength once more. 'It's going to be a cold night,' observed Jorina as she drove her little Citroën rather too fast along the icy road. 'You're sure you're happy to come back? It is your half day, you know.'

'Yes, I don't mind a bit,' said Julia. 'After all, I've been out the whole afternoon and what would I do with myself out on a night like this?'

'Go to Oisterwijk,' laughed Jorina. 'Oh, dear, Ivo was so worried about you when he got home—you should have seen him—and Marcia vexed because he said almost nothing to her...'

Julia interrupted hastily, 'Yes, it was so silly of me. I have enjoyed my afternoon, Jorina. Thank you for taking me.'

'I enjoyed it too. We'll do it again—there are still the Christmas presents to buy. We don't have such a gay time in Holland as you do in England because we have St Nikolaas first. But we do have a party and a tree and little gifts. You must wear that lovely pink dress you showed me.'

They talked clothes for the rest of the journey and went into the house, still talking, their faces glowing with the cold and the thought of Christmas ahead, and found Marcia sitting where they had left her with a book in her hand, gazing wistfully into the fire with a sad face which didn't deceive Julia one bit. She turned to look at them as they came in, pretending surprise, and remarked in a resigned voice,

'There you are—I'm sure you must have had a delightful time. How I wish I were able to enjoy the simple pleasures of life!'

Julia murmured encouraging as she glanced casually at the book in her patient's lap—and then glanced

again, for it was a different one from the volume of
Virgil Marcia had been reading when she and Jorina
had left; this one was a prosy tome on mediaeval
religion, twice as large as Virgil and with a different
coloured binding. When Jorina presently went from
the room Julia asked,

'Did Mijnheer de Winter come to see you, Miss
Jason?' and was rewarded by Marcia's slight flush
and frown.

'How strange that you should ask, nurse. As a matter of fact he did—to bring me another book.' She
went on in self-assured way, 'It was such a cold afternoon I persuaded him to stay and have tea with
me.'

'How nice—and now, if you're not tired, supposing
we walk around the house for a little while? There's
no one about and I daresay you're tired of sitting all
the afternoon.'

She saw the flush appear again. So Marcia hadn't
been sitting still all the afternoon! Julia, promenading
up and down the hall with her patient, tried to guess
what she was up to.

She was on the point of asking in a roundabout
fashion when Ivo came in from the hospital and Marcia, never one to miss an opportunity to attract attention to herself, cried,

'Oh Ivo, look at little me—aren't I splendid? I feel
so small and fragile and I'm sure I should fall over
if it were not for Nurse Pennyfeather's arm—isn't it
fortunate that she's such a stoutly built girl?'

Ivo threw off his coat, saying good evening as he
did so, then, with the faintest hint of a smile, he
turned to study Julia.

'No,' he said mildly, 'not stoutly built—shapely if you like, curvy if I am permitted to say so, but definitely not stout.'

Julia gave an enchanting gurgle of laughter. 'What a relief! I was beginning to feel like the village blacksmith.'

His smile widened. 'I can think of nothing less like,' he said, and they laughed at each other across the hall and Marcia, her well-modulated voice a little sharp, asked, 'Have you had a busy day, Ivo? I daresay your patients have been difficult...'

He was still looking at Julia, but now he turned politely to face her. 'No, not in the least, for the greater part of the time they're under the anaesthetic.' He looked at Julia again. 'Did you have a good time in Tilburg? But surely you should have the evening free as well?'

Julia tried not to look too pleased because he had remembered to ask.

'Lovely, thank you. Yes, I should be free, I suppose, but I'm quite happy about it—there's nothing for me to do on an evening like his.'

They were sitting down to dinner when Ivo said,

'No one minds if I take Julia to the cinema in Oisterwijk, do they?' He looked round the table at his father's and sister's approving faces, Marcia's affronted stare and Julia's astonished one. 'It's her half day,' he added blandly. 'I don't see why she should be forced to remain in—you agree, Marcia?'

'Well, of course—if Nurse wishes to go out she is entitled to, I suppose, although I should have thought a quiet evening with a book...'

Ivo was staring at her and Julia noticed that he had

his father's trick of lowering his lids so that it was hard to see his eyes.

'It's an old film,' he said mildly, turning to Julia. '*The Sound of Music*, if you can bear to see it again.'

'Oh, rather! I loved it.'

'A film I've never seen,' remarked Marcia tartly. 'A sentimental fairy tale, so I've been told.'

'Very sentimental,' agreed Ivo gravely, 'just the thing to round off a half day.'

Half an hour later, warmly coated and wearing the fur bonnet, Julia danced downstairs and into the sitting room, to stop short at the door. Ivo was standing just inside the room and Marcia was addressing him in the clear tones she affected and which Julia could not but hear.

'It's very good of you, Ivo, to sacrifice your evening in this way,' her patient was saying. 'I was looking forward to a pleasant conversation, but of course Nurse must have her amusement. I can only hope you won't be bored to tears.'

Julia stood in the hall and said to Ivo's back, 'I'm ready,' in a rather small voice. He turned and raked her with a bright glance before bidding Marcia goodnight and closing the door behind him. The moment he had done so, Julia said urgently, 'I couldn't help hearing—I—I didn't think—I wouldn't dream of spoiling your evening.'

He tucked her arm firmly into his. 'The only way my evening will be spoilt is if you don't come. It's just exactly what I need after a hard day's work.' He smiled as he spoke and ushered her into the car and got in beside her. 'The cinema's small,' he went on easily, 'and the audience is sometimes noisy—will you mind?'

'No,' said Julia happily, and meant it.

They had seats at the back of the crowded hall; they were narrow and not very well-sprung, and her companion by reason of his size was very close. It seemed the most natural thing in the world for him to take her hand in his and hold it throughout the performance. Even when the lights went up half way through, he didn't let go and she was content to let it remain there.

It was bitterly cold when they came out of the cinema and Ivo said, 'Coffee, I think, don't you?' and swept her across the street to Dc Wapen van Oisterwijk, where in an atmosphere redolent of the evening's dinner, cigars and the faint sharp tang of Genever, they sat in the pleasant little coffee room.

'The film was marvellous,' said Julia. 'Thank you for taking me. I don't suppose it was quite your cup of tea, though?'

'My what?' Ivo stared at her over his cup, 'Oh, I see—aren't men sentimental?'

'I don't know. I've never known one well enough to ask. But wasn't it a bit lowbrow for you?'

A muscle twitched at the corner of Ivo's mouth. 'No. Don't you know James well cnough to ask him?'

She shook her head. 'No. Besides, he's not the sort of person you'd ask.'

'Then you'd better not marry him.' He spoke lightly. 'If you've finished perhaps we had better go.'

She looked idly at the clock on the wall behind him and gasped,

'It's after eleven, Ivo! I should have been back ages

ago—what will Miss Jason do? How will she get to bed? I should never…'

'Panicking, Miss Pennyfeather?' His look was mocking. 'It's your half day, isn't it? I asked Jorina to help Marcia to bed—she can, you know, and I fancy that Marcia has become stronger in this last week—you must be having a good effect upon her.'

They were walking back to the car and he had tucked her arm in his again. 'I thought so too,' said Julia soberly. 'I wondered'—she hesitated—'I wondered if she were to go out in the car—you know, for a short trip or to see the shops—if she would enjoy it. Just to drive through a town when the shops are lighted up would make a change for her. I'm sure she's well enough.'

She didn't look at him as she spoke because she didn't want to see pleasure at the idea on his face. It wasn't until they were sitting in the car that he asked, 'You think that would be a good idea?'

She looked at him, a little puzzled because his voice had sounded almost reluctant. 'Well, you could ask her,' she suggested tentatively. 'It's almost Christmas; she might like to buy some presents.'

'So she might. And you, when will you buy yours?'

It seemed as though he didn't want to talk about Marcia. Julia said lightly, 'I've got some already, and I shall get the rest when I go into Tilburg again.'

He started the car. 'Very well, I'll take you both in one day next week—will that do?'

'Yes, but…'

'But what, Miss Pennyfeather?'

'Well, will you suggest it to Miss Jason and when she says yes, you could ask me as a kind of afterthought—otherwise it might look as though we'd arranged it all first and that might hurt her feelings.'

He made a small sound which could have been a laugh. 'If I were James I should come after you and marry you out of hand, my dear Miss Pennyfeather.'

'Why? And why do you call me Miss Pennyfeather?'

'You don't like it? But I always think of you as the magnificent Miss Pennyfeather. You are, you know, and you're not only quite beautiful, you're—alive.'

He stopped the car in front of the house, turned towards her, slid an arm around her shoulders and kissed her hard.

When she had her breath again she said with a kind of stunned politeness, 'Thank you for a very nice evening, Ivo.'

His face was only an inch or two from her own and he was smiling a little. 'I haven't enjoyed myself so much for a long time,' he said softly. 'No, that's not quite true. I enjoyed every minute of our stay at Drumlochie House.'

He got out and walked round the car's bonnet and opened the door for her. She went inside without saying anything more, only a quiet goodnight as she went up the stairs.

Her patient's light was still on. Julia pushed the half open door a little wider and looked into the room. Marcia was in bed with a book open in front of her. She said with gentle resignation,

'So you're back, Nurse Pennyfeather. The performance must have been a long one.' Her pale eyes searched Julia's vivid face. 'You look as though you've enjoyed yourself, but I hope you won't make a habit of this—I had the greatest difficulty in getting up the stairs.'

'I'm sorry,' said Julia, not sorry at all and at the same time appalled at her own feelings. She should be feeling guilty; spending the evening with Ivo while his Marcia lay in bed, only she didn't, because she was so very sure that Marcia didn't love Ivo, and she was almost as sure that Ivo didn't love Marcia, only perhaps he hadn't realised it yet. She said now, 'You managed very well by yourself yesterday—perhaps you were a little nervous.'

Marcia picked up her book. 'I'm never nervous,' she stated repressively. 'Now I'm sure you want to go to bed; you must be tired.'

'Not a bit,' said Julia comfortably. 'How can enjoying oneself make one tired? The film was delightful, you know, after these peculiar modern ones. I'll go and get ready for bed and then come back in case you might want something.'

But when she went back in half an hour's time, Marcia's light was out.

It was the following evening when Ivo broached the subject of Christmas. 'Shall we give our usual party?' he asked Jorina. 'Christmas Eve, I think, don't you? Marcia will be able to enjoy it.' He turned to look at her. 'You might even like to dance a few steps.'

'Naturally I shall do my best to enter into the spirit of Christmas,' Marcia was at her most gracious. 'And if you ask me, Ivo, I'm sure I'll have the strength to take a few steps of a slow foxtrot.'

Julia kept her eyes on the cloth she was embroi-

Play the
"LAS VEGAS"
GAME
GET 3 FREE GIFTS!
FREE GIFTS!
FREE GIFTS!
FREE GIFTS!
TURN THE PAGE TO PLAY!
Details inside!

Play the
"LAS VEGAS"
and get Game
3 FREE GIFTS!

FREE GIFTS!

FREE GIFTS!

1. Pull back all 3 tabs on the card at right. Then check the claim chart to see what we have for you — 2 FREE BOOKS and a gift — ALL YOURS! ALL FREE!

2. Send back this card and you'll receive brand-new Harlequin Romance® novels. These books have a cover price of $3.99 each in the U.S. and $4.50 each in Canada, but they are yours to keep absolutely free.

3. There's no catch. You're under no obligation to buy anything. We charge nothing — ZERO — for your first shipment. And you don't have to make any minimum number of purchases — not even one!

4. The fact is, thousands of readers enjoy receiving their books by mail from the Harlequin Reader Service®. They enjoy the convenience of home delivery...they like getting the best new novels at discount prices, BEFORE they're available in stores...and they love their *Heart to Heart* newsletter featuring author news, horoscopes, recipes, book reviews and much more

5. We hope that after receiving your free books you'll want to remain a subscriber. But the choice is yours — to continue or cancel, any time at all! So why not take us up on our invitation, with no risk of any kind. You'll be glad you did!

Visit us online at
www.eHarlequin.com

▶ DETACH AND MAIL TODAY ▶

Play the
"LAS VEGAS" Game

YES! I have pulled back the 3 tabs. Please send me all the free Harlequin Romance® books and the gift for which I qualify. I understand that I am under no obligation to purchase any books, as explained on the back and opposite page.

386 HDL DFSV

186 HDL DFSU
(H-RB-0S-10/01)

NAME   (PLEASE PRINT CLEARLY)

ADDRESS

APT.#   CITY

STATE/PROV.   ZIP/POSTAL CODE

GET 2 FREE BOOKS & A FREE MYSTERY GIFT!

GET 2 FREE BOOKS!

GET 1 FREE BOOK!

TRY AGAIN!

The Harlequin Reader Service®—Here's how it works:

BUSINESS REPLY MAIL
FIRST-CLASS MAIL   PERMIT NO. 717-003   BUFFALO, NY

POSTAGE WILL BE PAID BY ADDRESSEE

HARLEQUIN READER SERVICE
3010 WALDEN AVE
PO BOX 1867
BUFFALO NY 14240-9952

NO POSTAGE
NECESSARY
IF MAILED
IN THE
UNITED STATES

dering; someone ought to tell her patient that the slow foxtrot wasn't often danced these days. No one did; Ivo said merely in his kind way, 'That will be delightful. And what about shopping? I'm sure you are well enough to come into Tilburg with me one day and choose your presents. It will only be a question of crossing the pavement from the car to the shop. We could manage that—better still, let us take Julia with us to make it easier for you.'

Julia chose a strand of silk with care, threaded her needle and took a few stitches, waiting for Marcia's reply.

'Oh, presents—I'd almost forgotten about them. Am I really strong enough? It would be very pleasant, provided you don't let me get tired.' She laughed her little tinkling laugh. 'How silly I am to say that, for you wouldn't do that, would you, Ivo?'

'No, certainly not, I've had too much to do with polio cases.'

And that, thought Julia judiciously, wasn't what Marcia had meant at all. She said aloud, 'Yes, of course I'll come if you think it would help at all. It might save Miss Jason unnecessary fuss if I hold the parcels and so on.'

So it was arranged, and an afternoon two days ahead was set aside for the expedition, giving Marcia, as Julia pointed out, plenty of time to decide what she wanted to buy.

Mijnheer de Winter came the next morning while everyone but Julia was out. She left him sitting with Marcia and went to fetch him some coffee, as they had just had theirs. Marcia had greeted him with unconcealed pleasure; apparently she still lived in the days when servants—and Julia had no doubt in her mind that she ranked as that in her patient's eyes— were like furniture, neither seeing nor hearing. Julia went slowly down to the kitchen, her thoughts centred on the look Marcia had exchanged with her visitor and the length of their handclasp. She poured the coffee, put it on a tray and bore it upstairs, wondering as she went what Ivo thought of this odd friendship. He didn't strike her as the kind of man who would take kindly to playing second fiddle to anyone else, especially when it concerned the woman he was going to marry. She loitered on the landing, struck by the thought that she had never actually heard him say that he was going to marry Marcia. Nor, for that matter, had Marcia said so, although she had been quick enough to let Julia know that was what she expected.

Julia took in the rapidly cooling coffee, set it tidily on the table by Mijnheer de Winter's chair and retired to the desk in the window where she kept her charts and reports, but she had barely reached it when Marcia said gently, 'Oh, Nurse, do go and have half an hour to yourself. I shall be quite all right, and you must have so much to do.'

Julia went downstairs again; contrary to her patient's supposition she had nothing to do. She began to wander round the hall, studying the pictures. She was outstaring the penetrating and beady black eyes of a tyrannical old lady in a plum-coloured dress with a bustles, when the front door opened and Ivo came in. Her first sensation was one of delight at seeing him, the second of apprehension in case he went bounding upstairs before she had a chance to mention—oh, so casually—that Mijnheer de Winter had got there first. He cast his coat down rather untidily on the nearest chair, said hullo and then, 'I had no idea that my appearance had the power to make you look like that.'

'Like what?' asked Julia, playing for time.

'As though I'd caught you in the middle of some heinous crime. Have I?'

Julia laughed hollowly. 'No, of course not. You surprised me.'

He was standing just inside the door, and although his eyes were neither black nor beady, it was obvious that the old lady with the bustle had handed on the penetrating stare.

'Whose car is that outside?' he asked.

She should have been ready for that question; instead she uttered,

'Well—that is…'

He put his hands in his pockets and leaned comfortably against the wall, all day at his disposal. 'Do tell,' he invited silkily.

'Of course I'll tell,' she said crossly. 'It's no secret—it's Mijnheer de Winter's.'

He repeated the name. 'Do I know him?' he inquired.

'How should I know?' snapped Julia, getting more and more cross. If only the wretched little man would come downstairs and answer Ivo's questions for himself!

'Visiting Marcia?' Ivo's voice was very smooth. 'In that case I'll go up and see for myself, since you're so charmingly ill-tempered and secretive.'

He went upstairs unhurriedly without giving her time to answer, which was just as well, because she had nothing to say. She didn't think he was going to like Marcia's visitor, nor was he going to like Marcia forgetting to mention his visits, especially as she harped continuously upon her loneliness—almost, it had seemed to Julia, reproaching Ivo with it. She went into the kitchen and put the coffee on again, then wandered round the house, not quite liking to go upstairs but wondering if it would help if she did. She had just made up her mind to do so when she heard steps on the staircase and Ivo's voice, speaking with the icy civility of a well-mannered man determined not to show his illhumour. The front door opened and shut and a moment later Ivo lounged through the kitchen door.

'What a detestable fellow,' he remarked. 'No wonder you didn't want me to meet him.' He shot her a sudden fierce glance. 'And it seems that I knew all about him, or so. Marcia told me just now.'

Julia said quickly, 'I daresay if you were busy you might have forgotten—it's not important, is it—and if you had other things on your mind...'

'I had nothing important on my mind until a short time ago, and I should make it plain to you that I seldom forget anything which I am told.' He grinned suddenly. 'Aren't you going to offer me some coffee?'

She had a cup with him, there in the kitchen while he told that he was unexpectedly free because the surgeon who was to have taken the list had 'flu.

'Do you have a list this afternoon?' asked Julia.

'In Breda, yes. A pity you aren't free, I'd take you with me.'

She had been unable to prevent the look of pleasure

on her face, although she said quietly enough, 'That would have been pleasant, but I think it's a bit too far for Miss Jason, don't you?' and instantly wished she hadn't said it because his face hardened into a grimness which she couldn't bear to see. Before she could stop herself she asked impulsively, 'Can I help, Ivo—is—is something the matter?'

He passed his coffee cup, his face once more smoothly bland. 'You're the last one to help me, dear girl,' he said lightly. 'Is there any more coffee?'

She felt snubbed. She supposed he had fallen out with his Marcia, in which case, she thought crossly, it was his own affair. She left him to his coffee and went upstairs to her patient, who looked up as she went in and said with a roguish smile, 'There you are, nurse. Oh dear, how awkward that Ivo should come home while August was here. I'm sure he's not a jealous man—no more than any man would be in the circumstances,' she simpered at Julia, who felt sick, wondering how Ivo could bear the girl, 'but I must tell you a little secret, just between us girls. I've never mentioned Aug—Mijnheer de Winter to Ivo, there seemed no need, so I pretended that I had written and told him about his visits. I flatter myself that my quick thinking saved the situation.' She smiled, her eyes wary. 'Don't you agree?'

'No,' said Julia instantly, 'I don't. I can't think why you should have to tell a lie about something so trivial. Jorina thinks that Ivo knows about him too, so you must have told her the same tale—you ever said something of the sort to me. I can't see any reason for deceit.'

She crossed the room and picked up Marcia's walking stick and handed it to her silently. It was more than likely that her patient would dismiss her on the spot. She did no such thing, however. 'One can see, Nurse Pennyfeather,' she said archly, 'that you've never been in love.'

Julia resisted an impulse to give her patient a poke with the stick where it would hurt most. She was a little tired of being patronised by someone so foolishly out of date as Miss Jason.

'Are you engaged to Ivo?' she asked, and was astonished at herself for asking it.

Marcia looked outraged; Julia, watching her, thought that her pale prettiness masked a petty nature and that none of her feelings, good or bad, ran deep.

'My dear nurse, that's rather a personal matter, but since you have made it your business to ask, we have an understanding—before Ivo went to Edinburgh, indeed, before I was stricken down.'

Julia felt rage and sorrow working strongly under her neat uniform; she damped them down firmly. 'In that case,' she said briskly, 'it's a very good thing that you aren't stricken any longer. Another few weeks and you should be ready to go down the aisle.'

Marcia cast her a well-bred look of loathing. 'Nurse Pennyfeather, I don't care for vulgar remarks such as that.'

'Vulgar?' asked Julia, the bit well between her nice regular white teeth. 'What's vulgar about getting married? Now, if I'd proposed getting you fit enough to live in sin...'

Miss Jason, forgetting that she was still a semi-invalid walked quite briskly across the room. She hissed: 'You coarse, over-blown creature!'

'I feel sure you will apologise, Marcia,' said Ivo from the door. His voice was steely, so were his eyes. 'I am aware that you did not mean that, but if it was a joke, you'll be the first to agree with me that it was in very poor taste.'

Julia kept her back to him. 'It's quite all right,' she said matter-of-factly, 'Miss Jason was—was joking. Did you see how well she walked across the room without her stick?' She added a little breathlessly: 'It was my fault—I was joking about your wedding, and I had no right to do it.'

She swung round to face him and was shocked at the dark look on his face, although his voice was calm enough. 'In that case, you can cry quits, I imagine. Yes, Marcia, saw you walking—how clever of you to keep it a secret from us all. Another few days and you will be fit to travel.'

Marcia said quickly in a small soft voice, 'Oh, Ivo, I couldn't possibly do it again. I can't think what happened, but I feel so weak and helpless now.' Whereupon Julia, her feelings still much inflamed, put down the stick and said in a well-controlled voice,

'In that case, I'm sure the doctor will be only too glad to help you—I'll go on down and get your chair ready.'

She smiled bleakly at them both and whisked through the door without waiting for them to answer.

Lunch was a little difficult. Julia, who would have preferred to have gone to her room and had a good cry, did her best, but Marcia remained stonily polite, answering when she was spoken to but making no remarks of her own volition; in anyone else it would be sulking, but somehow she managed to convey a

sad air of dolour which effectively damped everyone's efforts to keep the conversation light. Julia rose
from the table with a sense of relief, and having seen
her patient settled for the afternoon in the sitting
room, begged to be excused. It was time for her three
hours' freedom—she intended taking a long walk; the
exercise would tire her out nicely and at the same
time allow her to think. She flung on her clothes with
little regard to her appearance and flew downstairs
and out of the door straight into Ivo, waiting on the
other side. He said mildly, 'I'll give you a lift. You're
not due back until about five, I gather?'

Julia nodded, twitching her fur bonnet straight and
tugging on her gloves. 'But I don't want a lift—I'm
going for a walk.'

As though she were a refractory child, he answered,
'Oh, nonsense,' caught her by the arm and marched
her to the car and bundled her in briskly, paying no
attention when she reiterated, 'I'm going for a walk,'
but getting in beside her and driving off in the direction of Oisterwijk. It was only when they were
through its main street, on the road to Tilburg, that
she ventured to ask, 'Where are we going?'

'I told you—I've a couple of cases in Breda this
afternoon.'

She looked at him with something like horror. 'But
that's miles away!'

'Your geography is sadly at fault, you'll have to
study a map. Breda is fifteen miles from Tilburg,
which we are rapidly approaching. It's half past one,
the list is at two o'clock, so we have plenty of time.
Why were you in such a hurry?'

'I—I wanted some fresh air.'

He was looking straight ahead, driving fast as he always did, with a nonchalance which was deceiving until you looked at the speedometer.

'I'm sorry Marcia upset you this morning. You must forgive her, she's been very ill.'

'It didn't matter, really it didn't,' she found herself protesting too much. 'She must hate being so inactive.' As she said it she remembered very clearly how well Marcia had walked across the room, and he had seen it too, although she had been clever enough to pretend it was a flash in the pan. Julia went on quickly, 'Miss Jason has quite a lot of shopping to do in Tilburg—it should be fun.'

A stupid remark, she thought, and he must have thought so too, for he didn't bother to reply, but as the outskirts of Breda closed in on them he said suddenly, 'I think we must plan a really merry Christmas, don't you? What a pity we can't keep it up until Twelfth Night, as they used to. What is that poem in English, something about "The first day of Christmas…"'

Julia obliged with a few verses, and when she got to the fifth day, stopped to remark. 'Five gold rings is a bit much, you know. Where would she wear them?'

'I shouldn't think it mattered; obviously her true love wanted to make certain that she knew he loved her.'

'Oh, well, there couldn't be much doubt about that, could there?' said Julia, once more lighthearted. 'I mean, one ring would be nice, but five—what more could any girl want?'

He didn't answer because they had stopped by the

Casualty entrance at the hospital. 'Hop out, dear girl,' he said. 'I'll take you to Zuster Bos before I go up to theatre.'

Zuster Bos was middle-aged and round; she had round blue eyes to match her rotund person and a delightful smile. She nodded vigorously to all that Ivo had to say, chuckled, shook Julia by the hand, said in quaintly accented English, 'Go away, bad boy,' and turned her attention to her guest.

Casualty was almost empty; the accidents, said Zuster Bos in difficult English helped out with a good deal of miming, were more frequent in the morning when the workers were still sleepy and perhaps a little careless—and the evening, when they were tired.

'Are you busy here?' asked Julia, prepared to enjoy herself.

'The book,' said Zuster Bos, and led her over to a desk at which a nurse sat writing. She looked up and smiled as they approached and handed over the Day Book, which Julia saw was exactly the same as the one in her own hospital, only the entries were in Dutch. But she could see the number of entries that it was a busy unit and would have enjoyed trying to decipher the various cases, but her mentor plucked her arm and led her to the office where she found herself drinking a cup of coffee and answering, in her turn, a great many questions about her own work. She said politely, 'Your English is very good Sister,' and was rewarded by a beaming smile.

'Yes? I learn in the war—I was young girl, but I nurse...' She paused, at a loss for a word.

'Men who escaped?' tried Julia, and watched the little woman's brow clear. 'Yes, they speak no

Dutch—I speak English.' She shrugged her plump shoulders and laughed cosily. It was a pity that at that moment an ambulance should shrill its way to the entrance and she had to go. But not for long. 'Not bad,' she announced as she sat down once more, 'Zuster van Rijk and Zuster Laagemaat can do all. It is,' she paused again, 'too much drug.'

'An overdose?' Julia guessed. 'Do you get a lot too? So do we.'

They talked happily together, helping each other when they came to words they didn't know. They were absorbed in the technique of resuscitation when Ivo came back. Julia watched him walking through Cas to the office. The nurses looked at him as they passed and he greeted them pleasantly without noticing their admiring glances. He looked relaxed and cheerful and very good-looking indeed. Julia turned her face away in case the admiration on her face showed too.

She was sorry to leave Zuster Bos, but as Ivo pointed out, it was already after half past two. He took her round the hospital, as he had promised, strolling from ward to ward where she was greeted more often than not in her own language and with a degree of friendliness she hadn't expected.

They walked back to the entrance. 'Is Tilburg hospital like this one?'

'Very similar. I go to Eindhoven sometimes, there's a splendid one there, and s'Hertogenbosch.'

'Where?'

He laughed and repeated the name, and standing in the hospital entrance oblivious of curious passers-by, made her repeat it too until she had it right, and only then did they get into the car again. They were outside the town when Julia saw a signpost to Roosendaal and remarked that she had thought that town to be in the opposite direction to Tilburg.

'And so it is, but you don't suppose I can travel any farther without tea, do you?' He glanced at her. 'Don't fidget, we've plenty of time. There's a place at Princenhage, just along this road.'

They stopped at the Mirabelle restaurant and went inside to a warmth very welcome after the cold outside. They had tea, each with their own little pot which amused Julia very much, and some rich and elaborate cakes, which, she declared, were a shame to eat, although she contradicted her words by eating hers to the last crumb, and when pressed to have a second, did so. She licked a morsel of cream off her pretty mouth with the tip of her tongue and sighed contentedly. 'I oughtn't to have them,' she said, although the remark was purely rhetoric, 'I shall get fat.'

He smiled lazily at her across the table. 'Never,' he said. 'You'll stay as you are for ever and ever.'

Julia pushed back her chair and put on her gloves and said lightly to cover her feelings, 'So now I'm indestructible as well as stoutly built!' and giggled so infectiously that he laughed too.

The shopping expedition the next day was, on the whole, a success. Marcia, well wrapped against the cold, was as excited as she would allow herself to be and even though it turned out that most of the shopping was for herself, it was pleasant to spend most of the afternoon in the bigger stores, even though her insistence on being treated as an invalid became a little irksome towards the end. Only once did she show any desire to do anything for herself and that was to post a handful of letters, something in which she was frustrated by Ivo, despite her protests. Julia, watching him putting them into the letter box, saw that he was looking at each of them in turn; she knew when he saw the one addressed to Mijnheer de Winter because of his quick frown. He said nothing, however, and nothing in his manner indicated that he was annoyed, although she caught Marcia's faintly worried look. Possibly Ivo had asked her not to continue her friendship with de Winter, but they weren't likely to discuss it before her. They had tea presently and Ivo was at his most amusing and if anything, kinder and more considerate of Marcia than he had been before. Julia, sitting in the back of the car on their way home, watched him in the gloom, bending his head to hear what Marcia had to say, and when Marcia laughed, which was often, Julia clenched her hands tightly in her lap, hurting them, as if by doing so she could ease the hurt in her heart.

She avoided him for the next day or two, and although they saw each other at meals and in the sitting room there was always someone else there. And on the third day, when she was free after one o'clock, she walked into Oisterwijk and did her Christmas shopping; a quite handsome coffret of eau de Cologne for Marcia, a tobacco pouch for Doctor van den Werff, handkerchiefs—fine linen ones—for Ivo and for Jorina some French soap as well as the teacloth she had embroidered. For Bep she found a scarf and for the girl who came up from the village every day

to work, a box of chocolates. She went straight to her
room when she got back, did up her parcels and put
them away at the back of the big cupboard in her
bedroom, then went down to dinner. It was during
that meal that Doctor van den Werff remarked,

'It seems to me that Julia has a very bad bargain
for her half day; it is in fact no half day at all. Here
she is, back here with us, whether she likes it or not,
because there's nothing for her to do.' He looked
across the table at her, smiling. 'Do you mind, Julia?'

She smiled back, 'No, not at all. I've letters to write
and those will take me all the evening. I had a nice
afternoon in Oisterwijk too. One day when it's fine,
I shall go for a long walk.'

Ivo looked up from the pear he was peeling for
Marcia. 'Well take care if you do, there's quite a lot
of fen country around here and this time of year it's
rough underfoot.'

Julia thanked him politely and lapsed into silence
once more while Marcia, with a sad little smile, wondered out aloud and at some length when she would
be able to go for a long walk—or, she added bravely,
if she ever would again.

'I can't see why not,' said Julia kindly. 'Why not
come into the garden with me tomorrow morning?
We needn't go far and the worst that can happen is
for you to fall over, when I shall pick you up again.'

They all laughed except Marcia, who flushed
faintly and said gently,

'How kind of you to offer, nurse, but I couldn't
trust myself to you—I need someone big and strong.'
She glanced at Ivo as she spoke and he said placidly,
'That sounds like me, but unfortunately I'm going

away for a couple of days.' He looked up briefly. 'I can't see what harm there would be in going with Julia as long as there's no ice about—you said yourself she was robust.'

Julia, who had just taken some wine, choked on it, laughing. 'I'll never live that down, shall I?' she declared cheerfully.

She went back to her room as soon as dinner was over because she felt that they expected her to, but once there she wrote no letters at all, for the only one she had to answer was an angry one from her brother, full of approaches and pointing out how selfish she had become. She sat, instead, in a chair, doing nothing until bedtime. She heard Marcia, with Ivo as escort, come upstairs and there Jorina to make sure Marcia was safely in bed. She felt a fraud, sitting there doing nothing and being paid handsomely for it. They would surely send her back to England directly after Christmas. She went on sitting idly, long after the others came to bed. Ivo was last of all; she heard him in the garden with Ben and then presently come indoors again. The house was quite silent when at last she went to bed herself.

CHAPTER SIX

THE OPPORTUNITY to go for a walk came sooner than
Julia had expected, for two days later Ivo, back from
wherever he had been, took Marcia into Tilburg in
the morning. She had complained with her usual
steely gentleness that her hair looked terrible, adding
at the same time that she quite understood that no one
could spare the time to take her to the hairdresser, but
when Julia had immediately offered to go with her
and Jorina had offered to drive them she refused on
the grounds that she was selfishly taking up their time.
It was inevitable that she contrived to tell Ivo in such
a way that she gained his instant attention and the
promise to take her himself on his way to hospital,
and when Julia had asked if she was to go too, Marcia
had said quite cheerfully, having gained her own
ends,

'Of course not, Nurse Pennyfeather—you may
have your free time this morning, that will make a
nice change for you.' Whereupon Ivo had said, 'Why
not have a lift in with us, Julia? There must be something you can amuse yourself with for a couple of
hours.'

But Julia had declined because she considered he
had listened too readily to Marcia's curdled account
of her efforts to get to the hairdresser while he was
away—besides, the less she saw of him the better.
She had thanked him politely in a serene voice which

betrayed nothing of her true feelings and declared her intention of taking a walk.

She tried not to think about Ivo and Marcia while she changed into her outdoor clothes. It was cold and a little misty outside and the sky was a mass of thick grey clouds, but there was always the chance that the sun would shine. She tucked a scarf into the neck of her top coat and tied the fur bonnet securely. She had studied a local map the previous evening and knew just where she was going. She ran downstairs and put her head round the kitchen door, called goodbye to Jorina and went out of the house.

The heath stretched away beyond the woods behind the house, and according to the map, it was criss-crossed by bicycle paths. She intended to take one of these as far as the village of Breukelen about three miles away and then return along another of the paths.

The wind stung her cheeks and whipped her black hair from under her bonnet, but it was exhilarating and the exercise did her good, and presently, glowing with warmth, she slowed her pace a little the better to think. She would have to go back to England soon—after Christmas, she thought, and if Marcia was going home shortly, would it not be a good idea if they were to travel together. But was Marcia going home? She had said nothing to that effect; perhaps she intended to remain until she married Ivo. The thought of it made Julia catch her breath and was swamped by the idea she had kept buried until now. Ivo wasn't in love with Marcia; he didn't want to marry her, although perhaps he had been attracted to her when they first met, for she was undoubtedly a very clever girl and in her way attractive too, but the pity he had shown her when she was taken ill had been mistakenly—or deliberately?—misconstrued as love by Marcia and he had been unable to let her see that she was wrong because she had been so ill. Perhaps he had thought that an absence of six months would terminate the affair in a gentler fashion. But it hadn't, or so it seemed to Ivo at least, and Julia had the uneasy suspicion that if he thought that Marcia still loved him he would never do anything to hurt her because in some way Marcia had made him feel responsible for her illness. Julia was certain that this wasn't the case, but she had no proof. It was a pity that Ivo held such lofty principles. She said loudly in exasperation, 'Old-fashioned bunkum—no one behaves like that any more,' and knew even as she said it that Ivo did.

She began to walk faster as if to get away from her thoughts, and when she came to a fork in the path, took the right-hand one without really noticing. It was some time later when she realised that she must have taken the wrong direction, for by now she should have reached the village. She stood still, trying to get her bearings, and decided that the path would probably end at some houses at least. But it didn't; she had walked steadily for some time now and it had no end, she stopped again and felt the first drops of freezing rain sting her face. She hadn't noticed that the sky, already grey, had become almost black behind her, and she would have to find shelter as quickly as possible. There were woods to the right of her. She looked at them carefully and decided that they must be part of the woods she had walked through when she had started out—if so, she had only to reach them and then walk in their shelter in the direction she had come from.

With the rain had come a gale of wind, whistling through the trees so that their branches creaked and groaned about her head, caring twigs and smaller branches with it. She was tired by now and very cold as well as hungry, and once or twice, in the dimness under the trees, she fell. It was only too apparent that she was lost, and in the blinding rain, even if she ventured away from the woods, she had little hope of finding her way. The sensible thing to do was to keep on walking; she knew from the map that the area of heath and fen land round Oisterwijk was a rough triangle, bounded by roads, so sooner or later, she was bound to strike one or other of them. Not too much later, she hoped, for it was after two o'clock now and getting dark, with the rain still pouring from an unbroken pall of cloud.

She went on walking, beginning to get a little frightened, for the night would be long and cold and although she would have liked to rest, she dared not in case she fell asleep. Someone would have missed her by now—Jorina or Bep. Doctor van den Werff would have been out on his rounds and wouldn't know anyway, and neither would Ivo, who would probably stay in Tilburg with Marcia until the weather cleared. She stumbled a little and fell into a small hollow between two fir trees. It was dry, covered in pine needles and sheltered from the wind. She hadn't meant to rest, but it was warmer there and surely five minutes wouldn't hurt. Julia sat down, drew her knees up under her chin, clasped her gloved hands round them and rested her head upon them. She was asleep within seconds.

She was roused by a hand on her shoulders, shaking her roughly awake. A voice—Ivo's voice—was telling her, equally roughly, that she was a damned little idiot. He pulled her to her feet, which were numb to the knees so that she lurched against him, and tore off her gloves to rub her cold hands.

'You fool!' he said violently, as he rubbed. 'Haven't you got the sense to keep moving in weather like this—and what possessed you to walk all these miles?'

He stopped his rubbing for a moment, flung an arm around her shoulders to hold her steady and poured some brandy down her throat in a ruthless fashion which left her spluttering and choking, and then resumed his work.

'Ugh!' uttered Julia, gaining strength from the brandy. 'Leave me alone—shouting at me like that. You're hurting me!'

He sat her down with a thump, pulled off a boot and started on her foot. When he spoke it was forcefully and in his own language. He sounded furious, and what with too much brandy on an empty stomach and pain from the reviving circulation of her hands she felt most peculiar. She said in a voice that choked a little, 'I got lost.'

He put the boot back on again, and took off the other one.

'What possessed you—' he began harshly, and then in a rigidly controlled voice: 'Jorina told me you left the house before eleven—do you know the time now?'

Julia gave a weak but spirited snort. 'How can I? It's dark. When I looked at my watch it was just after three, but that must be half an hour or so ago.'

He gave her a look of such fierceness through the gloom that she caught her breath. 'It's after six o'clock,' he said dryly.

She shivered violently. 'It can't be—I sat down for a minute.'

'It was pure chance that I found you—you know what would have happened if I hadn't?'

'Well, I suppose I should have gone on sleeping.'

'And died of exposure.' He sounded grim.

'I—I didn't think of that,' she faltered a little. 'Have you been looking for me for a long time?'

'Rub your hands together and then clap them. Since we got home at about one o'clock.'

Julia was stricken into silence. She ventured at last, 'Just you?'

'No. Until it became really dark and the weather got too bad, we all searched—which meant leaving Marcia alone in the house. We left this stretch of the woods until last because it didn't seem possible that you could get so far.'

She said stupidly, 'But I'm not far. I'm on my way back to your house. If I had walked straight on…'

'You would have eventually come to the village of Oirschot—ten kilometres from Oisterwijk—that is, if you had wakened up.'

'You must be mistaken.'

He put on her boot and stood her on her feet again and gave her a little shake. 'For God's sake stop arguing with me,' he said loudly, then caught her close and kissed her so fiercely that she had no breath.

'Fool,' he declared. 'Fool!' and let her go so suddenly that she almost fell. If her mind as well as her body hadn't been so numbed, she would most certainly have given this piece of rudeness the answer it so richly deserved, for she felt certain that it was directed against herself, but her teeth were chattering so much that she found it impossible to speak. She made a small, indignant noise and he said harshly,

'Too cold to talk, eh? That's a good thing, now I shan't have to listen to your excuses all the way home.' His voice was so furiously angry that Julia felt her eyes fill with tears and was thankful for the dark, but even as she had thought, he turned his torch on her face. She felt his arm round her once more, but this time it was gentle and comforting. He said in a quite different voice, 'Drink this, dear girl—I know you dislike it, but it will help to warm you.'

She swallowed obediently and the spirit's warmth crept over her, making her feel more cheerful as well as less cold, although the tears ran down her cheeks still. But she made no attempt to wipe them away, she had indeed forgotten them; she sniffed a little forlornly and began to walk wordlessly, urged on by his arm in the light from the torch. It seemed a long way to the car; she stumbled along beside him as he strode ahead, unworried by the rain and the wind and the blackness of the early evening, but presently they came with unexpected suddenness out of the woods and on to a road and she saw the Jensen's lights.

Ivo picked her up and tossed her into the seat beside his without a word, then got in beside her, and at the same time she became aware that Ben was in the car too, warm and doggy-smelling. He leaned his shaggy head over the back of her seat and licked her gently, then at a quiet word from Ivo, he slid between them to settle at her feet. Julia felt his solid warmth envelop her feet and legs and said through chattering teeth, 'Dear Ben...'

'He'll warm you up,' said Ivo in a perfectly ordinary voice as he wrapped a blanket around her shoulders. 'He wanted to come with me, but he's been looking for you too all the afternoon and he's—as you so aptly say—dog-tired.'

He didn't say any more, but turned the car with a good deal of skill on the icy road and started for home. The car skidded several times on the way back, but Julia, now that the effects of the brandy were wearing off, was feeling too miserable to notice anything as trivial—her thoughts were entirely of Ivo's anger with her. It had perhaps been foolish of her to have gone so far, but she hadn't got lost deliberately, it was something which could have happened to anyone. She said out loud,

'How intolerant you are!'

Ivo laughed, sounding amused and irritated too. 'You do me less than justice—at any moment now you will be telling me that it was my fault that you got lost.' He sighed. 'Didn't you look to see where you were going when you started out?'

Julia clutched Ben round the reassuring thickness of his neck as the car went into another skid. 'Of course I did, but I was thinking. I—I must have taken a wrong turning.'

'What were you thinking of, Julia?'

She said a little too quickly, 'I don't remember.'

'Liar,' he observed blandly, and didn't speak again

until they slid to a halt before the house. The door was opened before they had stopped, revealing Bep and behind her Doctor van den Werff and Jorina. Julia, still cold and stiff despite Ben's best efforts, was glad of Ivo's arm as they went inside, although she essayed a smile as the three of them crowded round her.

'A hot bath,' said Doctor van den Werff, 'a hot drink too. How do you feel, Julia? You poor child, I feel responsible.'

Julia, who had expected a scolding or at least reproaches for being so stupid, felt a strong desire to burst into tears again. Kindness was something she hadn't reckoned with and her voice wobbled a bit as she said, 'I'm sorry I was so silly and gave you all so much trouble,' and was patted and soothed by the three of them, but all Ivo did was to say, 'You'd better do as you're told or we shall have you sneezing over us all.'

She nodded without looking at him and followed Bep upstairs with Jorina, an arm round her waist, beside her. As they went she heard Ivo ask his father, 'Where's Marcia?' which had the effect of starting her tears again, to her own great surprise and when she mumbled an apology, Jorina said kindly, 'You're tired and I expect you were frightened too—I should have been—and it must have been very cold, yes?'

'Yes,' said Julia.

She went downstairs a couple of hours later, warm once more and looking exactly as she always did in her neat uniform, save for her beautiful face which was a little pale. They were all in the sitting room and while Ivo had nothing to say his father called to her to go and sit with him and asked her very kindly if she felt well enough to stay up. 'We put dinner back,' he explained, 'but you can just as easily have it in bed if you wish.'

Julia said shyly, 'That's very kind of you, doctor, but I feel quite well, thank you, only very foolish.' She glanced across the room to where Marcia was sitting by the fire. 'I'm so sorry, Miss Jason,' she began, 'for being such a nuisance—I hope I didn't spoil your day or cause you any inconvenience.'

Miss Jason bowed her head in graceful acknowledgement of this apology and said with a sickening graciousness, 'Well, I daresay it has taught you a lesson, nurse. You are, I imagine, an impetuous young woman, lacking the intellectual powers of the more intelligent person, who would have given all the aspects of a walk in the country at this time of year the deliberation they deserve.'

Julia took a few moments to unwind this prosy speech and make sense of it. She didn't care for it all; she was willing to admit that she had been at fault, but she wasn't going to be preached over. She opened her mouth to say so and was forestalled in the nick of time by Ivo, who said smoothly,

'Most unjust, Marcia, as well as making a great fuss about nothing. We have all been lost at some time or other, found, and brought home. There's nothing so special about going for a walk even at this time of year, and not all of us find it necessary to weigh the pros and cons before we do so.' He turned to Jorina and said easily,

'Do you remember the time you went to find St Nikolaas—how old were you? Five? You looked like a snowman when I found you and you kicked me all the way home because I wouldn't let you go on looking for him.' They laughed together and Jorina answered, 'And what about that time you felt sure you'd failed your exams and came in frozen stiff in the middle of my birthday party after Father found you walking round in circles?' She laughed across at Julia, seemingly unaware of the indignant look still on Julia's face. 'You've no idea what a horror Ivo was—still is. Is your brother like that?'

Julia smiled despite herself. Her brother was as unlike Ivo as chalk from the proverbial cheese. She shook her head. 'I can't remember him ever doing anything to give anyone a moment's unease.'

'The fellow sounds like a dead bore,' observed Ivo carelessly.

'He is.' She saw the little smile curl the corners of his mouth and added hastily, 'He's a very worthy sort of person.'

Ivo got up. 'I'll not attempt to compete,' he stated lightly. 'Who's for a drink?'

It was when, a moment or two later, he handed her a glass of sherry that she remembered, far too vividly, the brandy he had poured down her throat in such an unceremonious fashion a few hours previously, and flushed up to her eyes under his amused look. But he didn't say anything and presently went to sit by Marcia again, and Julia, to her secret satisfaction, couldn't help but notice that his manner towards her was a little cool.

There were still several days to Christmas; Julia spent them in encouraging her patient to overcome what slight disability remained; determined to atone for the nuisance she had been and doggedly accepting Miss Jason's chastening lectures, given in her gentle, modulated voice, which she delivered at least once a day, and if there was time, twice, so that presently Julia began to feel herself a slightly inferior being, only tolerated because of her patient's high-minded principles. Her common sense told her that this was not, indeed, the fact, but she was fast losing her self-assurance, especially as she saw very little of Ivo, and when she did, he treated her with a casual politeness which made it impossible to talk to him. Not that she had any desire to talk to him, she told herself vigorously; let him marry his wretched Marcia and take the consequences—in five years' time he would be as dreary as his wife; he would probably wear goloshes and never drive at more than forty miles an hour and they would have one, or worse, no children because Marcia would feel herself to be too delicate. Julia, making her patient's bed, thumped the pillows with quite unnecessary vigour.

It was that evening at dinner that Jorina announced that she intended going to the Hague the following day. Klaas was there for a couple of days, she said, and she would combine seeing him with some shopping.

'What sort of shopping?' her father wanted to know.

'Well, there's the party in two days' time, and I might see something I liked.' She turned to Julia. 'Come with me, its time you had a day to yourself. Besides, you'll see nothing of Holland before you go back.'

Julia agreed silently; she hadn't had a day off since

she had arrived and although she was paid a handsome salary, she would have liked the opportunity of spending some of it. All the same, it had been made clear to her when she accepted the job that she was to have two half days a week; nothing had been said about a whole day. She said now,

'Thank you, Jorina, but that would mean the whole day away, you know, and you would be away too—I can't leave Miss Jason alone.'

Doctor van den Werff put down his knife and fork. 'Why ever not?' he asked. 'Jorina won't be leaving until ten o'clock or thereabouts; plenty of time to get Marcia downstairs and Bep can do anything needed once she is down. You'll be back long before bedtime.' He smiled pleasantly at Marcia. 'You won't mind? It will be splendid practice for you, for you won't be needing a nurse much longer, you know. The quicker you become independent, the better, eh?'

Thus addressed, there was nothing Marcia could do but agree, albeit sourly, and she looked even more sour when Ivo said casually,

'I've no cases at the hospital tomorrow, how about going in my car? I think that's a better idea than you driving that tin box of yours, Jorina, and we'll get there much faster. Besides, the roads aren't too good and you never could cope with a skid. There are a number of things I want to do in the Hague.'

Jorina agreed so quickly that Marcia looked up suspiciously, but Ivo's face was merely blandly inquiring and Jorina looked so innocent that any doubts she had were discarded. And Julia listening to this exchange, had no doubts at all; even if Ivo spent the whole day going about his own business there was still the drive there and back. When he gave her an enquiring look she said at once, 'I should very much like to go. I've been reading a book about the Hague and there are several places I should like to see.'

The next morning saw very little improvement in the weather. A light frosting of snow had fallen during the night and the sky was leaden. Although she wasn't a nervous girl, Julia was glad that Ivo would be driving and not Jorina. She thought about it with pleasure as she got Marcia downstairs and comfortably settled with the day's paraphernalia around her. She was still thinking about it as she dressed herself with extra care. She hadn't many clothes with her, she put on the brown wool dress, covered it with her top-coat, arranged the fur bonnet upon her dark head, snatched up her gloves and handbag and danced downstairs. She hadn't seen Ivo that morning, and the awful thought that he might have changed his mind about driving to the Hague crossed her mind as she entered the sitting room.

He hadn't. He was sitting, ready dressed to go out, on the arm of a chair, reading the paper and carrying on a desultory conversation with Marcia while he did so. He put the paper down as Julia went in and said, 'Hullo, there you are. Jorina has gone to the kitchen to see Bep.' He got to his feet then swept her out of the room, saying over his shoulder as he went, 'Goodbye, Marcia—I'll do my best to get that book for you.'

Julia, gabbling farewells as they went, was walked across the hall and outside to where the car was waiting, but when he opened the door and said genially, 'Get in, dear girl,' she hung back and enquired if Jorina wouldn't prefer to sit in front, whereupon he gave her a little push with the remark, 'I've never met such a woman for arguing,' and shut the door upon her, then before she could think of a suitable answer Jorina arrived and got into the back of the car saying,

'Don't anyone talk to me until I say so—I'm making lists of food for the party. Ivo, you'll see to the drinks? I'll go into Lensvelt Nicola and get some petits fours…' There was a pause while she wrote busily. 'And there's that place in the Lange Vooruit where they sell those cheesy things, and I want some shoes and another handbag if I see one I like.'

They were already half way to Tilburg. 'Does Klaas come at the top or bottom of the list?' asked Ivo.

'Top, of course. If you drop me outside Metz—he said he's going to wait until I come. What are you going to do, Julia?'

'I'm going to the top of St Jacobskerk tower to see the view,' said Julia promptly, 'and then the Mauritshuis, and then I'm going to take a look at the Huis den Bosch. I can't go in, but all the same I'd like to see it.'

The rest of the journey passed pleasantly enough, and for Julia it was a delight, for she had Ivo beside her and just for a few hours she was determined to forget Marcia and her own imminent return to England. It was high time she made a few plans for her future, for she had nowhere to go, only to her brother's house, and he, although he would give her house room, would hardly welcome her with open arms after the way she had treated him. But it all seemed very far away from the flat, wintry landscape

they were passing through; she concentrated on studying the places of interest pointed out to her and joined
in the cheerful talk without giving a hint of her more
sombre thoughts.

The Hague, once they had reached the heart of the
city, was everything she had imagined an old Dutch
city to be, for although Tilburg had pleased her very
much and she had liked Breda, the Hague seemed,
once they were through the suburbs, like a city from
the Golden Age. They set Jorina down outside Metz,
a shop which Julia resolved to explore should she find
the time, and then went through the city to the Huis
den Bosch where Ivo stopped the car.

'Will this suit you?' he wanted to know cheerfully.
'You can't get lost—just follow the road back into
the city again.'

Julia looked behind her. 'But it's miles!'

'Oh no—two perhaps, no more.'

She eyed him a little uncertainly. 'Where—where
shall I meet you, then?'

'Now as to that, supposing we get out of the car
and you can take your fill of the Huis den Bosch as
we walk along and discuss it.'

He took her arm and marched her along briskly,
away from the main road, and Julia, having looked
her fill, said politely, 'Thank you, I've had a good
look.' She paused and went on a little apprehensively,

'If you would tell me your plans.'

He halted abruptly, and she with him. 'That's better. First you refuse to have lunch with me, and then
you try to brush me off... My plans depend upon you,
Julia. You'll waste a great deal of time on your own,
you know, and you may not get the chance to come

again. Supposing I take you back now and leave you in the Noordeinde—a shopping centre where you can't get lost. What I have to do won't take above an hour. I'll wait for you at the spot where I put you down presently. We'll have lunch and then go wherever you want. Jorina won't be ready until six o'clock.' Julia, before she could stop herself, said, 'Oh, how lovely!' and then, 'I shall be a nuisance to you—you said you had things to do.' She stared up at him, her eyes shining, her face eager, despite her words, to meet his own eyes, bright and intent and with an expression she couldn't read. An instant later she felt his arms around her.

'So I did,' he said calmly, 'and this was one of them,' and he bent his head to kiss her. And Julia, her common sense blown away by the winter wind whistling around them, kissed him back. Even as she did so, she was regretting it; she couldn't very well have prevented him from kissing her, but there was absolutely no need to return his kiss. She said as lightly as her voice would allow, 'What silly things one does at Christmas,' and even achieved a laugh with it as she slipped out of his arms, to feel immediately and illogically put out because he gave no sign of minding. She caught herself wondering how Marcia would have reacted; there was no way of telling what his own feelings were, although she fancied she could see amusement behind the calmness of his face.

He didn't answer her remark, only asked casually, 'Have you any shopping to do? Will an hour be long enough?'

'Oh, plenty,' said Julia. If he was going to be casual, she could be too. 'I don't intend to do much shopping, only look.'

He talked with a disarming friendliness as they drove to the centre of the city and left her, with strict instructions to be on that same spot in about an hour's time. Julia watched the Jensen slide away in the traffic and felt lost. But the shop windows were diverting, and she wandered along, wishing she could buy a great many of the things she saw, but beyond one or two trifles, she didn't dare because she would soon be out of work; even if she went back to her hospital, she wouldn't get any money for the rest of the month, and she didn't think her brother would think of paying her if she went there. She stared into the window of a tiny boutique, exhibiting in its window exactly the kind of party dress any girl would fall for. It had no price ticket, and presently she walked on, staring up at the old houses above the shops; it would be delightful to go into a shop like that and buy the dress without even asking the price. But it was the jewellers' shops which caught her attention. She looked in each one, and it was while she was feasting her eyes upon the contents of one of their windows that she saw Ivo coming out of an even more opulent jeweller's across the street. He was stuffing a small box into a pocket as he came through the door and judging from the satisfied look on the face of the man who had opened it for him, he had spent a lot of money…a ring for Marcia? A wedding ring? Julia turned her back upon both Ivo and her thoughts and plunged through the door before her, for if she didn't Ivo would surely see her.

She found herself in a richly furnished shop housing a great many showcases containing antique silver, diamond tiaras and suchlike expensive trifles. She gazed unhappily at a trio of diamond bracelets, displayed with studied carelessness upon dark blue velvet, and when a young man approached her and said something in Dutch she turned her pretty, worried face to his and said apologetically,

'I don't want to buy anything—there was someone I didn't want to meet...'

She looked so forlorn and so beautiful that he instantly dismissed the idea that she was a thieves' accomplice and smiled kindly at her.

'Please stay if you wish,' he said in quite beautiful English, and went to the door to study the street, and Julia came to peer over his shoulder. 'He's gone,' she breathed thankfully. 'I'll go—it was kind of you...'

He opened the door for her and she went out into the Noordeinde once more, to stare unseeingly at the shops until it was time to meet Ivo.

He was waiting for her, although she was a little early, but she could see no car. 'I haven't kept you waiting?' she asked. 'The shops are so delightful.'

He smiled and raised an eyebrow. 'And you have bought nothing? I find that a miracle. Jorina would have an armful of parcels by now.'

Julia smiled, wanting to point out that if she had the money his sister had at her disposal she would have no difficulty in rivalling her spending powers. Did he actually think that she didn't like clothes?

He must have guessed her thoughts, for he inquired, 'Didn't you see anything at all you would have liked to buy?'

She nodded. 'Any number. There was a dress—a

party dress with no price on it—an extravagant dress.' She added hastily because he made a sudden hasty movement and she was afraid he might insist on going back to look at it, and still worse, buy it, 'Not the kind of dress I could ever wear.'

He smiled and took her arm. 'That's an arguable point,' he observed. 'Now let's have a meal.'

They didn't have to walk far, round the corner into Molenstraat to the Park Hotel and into its restaurant over-looking the gardens of a former royal palace. Julia, who hadn't expected anything as grand, went away to take off her bonnet and returned, quite unconscious of the stares directed at her dark loveliness, to find that Ivo had ordered the drinks.

'I chose this place,' he explained, 'because it is close to most of the places you want to visit.'

He lifted a finger and the hovering wait   handed them menu cards and stepped back to a discreet distance. Julia studied hers with deep interest. As far as she could see, everything that anyone could possibly want was on it.

'A starter?' prompted Ivo. 'How about Mousse d'Avocat? If you like avocado pears.' Julia, who had never eaten one, had no intention of telling him so, she nodded and chose soufflé de Turbot Hollandaise, leaving him to decide upon quenelle of pike Nantua before going into conference with the wine waiter, but once the important question of what they were going to eat had been settled, he gave her his undivided attention.

'And what do you think of our shops?' he wanted to know.

'Super,' said Julia briefly, 'only expensive.' She was eating her avocado pear and finding it delicious.

He agreed. 'And of course it is Christmas—the shops show all their most tempting wares. Did you look at any jewellery?'

Julia kept her eyes on her plate and wished that she didn't flush so easily. 'Yes—they're marvellous. The diamonds!'

'You like diamonds?'

She was surprised into looking at him. 'Me? Of course—I imagine all women do.'

'A safe choice for a man to make, you think?' He sounded only casually interested.

Julia eyed her turbot with a sudden lack of appetite. 'Very safe,' she said, but surely he would have asked Marcia…? 'But women don't have to have diamonds, you know. I should think most of them are quite happy with—with turquoises or garnets or something similar.'

'Rubies?' he asked lightly, smiling.

So it was rubies for Marcia; Julia wondered if he knew that bit about a good woman being above rubies; probably not. She said woodenly,

'Definitely rubies,' and he went on to talk about something else. It was when they were eating dessert—mangoes in champagne—that he remarked, 'How delightful the meals were in Drumlochie House—I often think of them.'

Julia, full of false cheer from the wine and the champagne and Cointreau which had enwrapped the mangoes, smiled at him. 'Me too. But the meals weren't all that good, you know. I expect it was because we were all hungry for most of the time and cold as well.'

'Lord, yes. Those bedrooms—mine was like an ice house.'

She remembered him lying on the great bed, fast asleep, and smiled. 'You looked like a petrified knight on a tomb,' she said, and went a little pink when he said on a laugh, 'Did I? I shan't tell you what you looked like.'

She avoided his eye, concentrating on her coffee cup. The conversation was back on their old easy footing, and it wouldn't do. Marcia's long face floated in the air before her, looking reproachful, and much as Julia disliked her, she couldn't take advantage of her behind her back. She asked briskly, 'Where are we going first? And can you really spare the time?'

He assured her that he could and suggested the Ridderzaal, followed by a visit to the Mauritshuis museum, and lastly the tower of St Jacobskerk. If there was any time over from these treats he declared that he would see that no second of it was wasted. The afternoon arranged, they set off for the Ridderzaal, where the beamed roofs, stained glass windows and flags which adorned the walls of this thirteenth-century building satisfied even Julia's lively imagination. There weren't many visitors on such a cold afternoon, and the guide, about to conduct a handful of people round, asked without much interest if they wished to join his party, but Ivo, after a short parley, walked her off in the opposite direction to the one in which the guide was taking and they ambled around undisturbed and almost alone, while he explained the history of the old place at some length.

The museum was just behind the Ridderzaal, housed in a beautiful sixteenth-century house. Here they dawdled amongst the Rembrandts, Vermeers, Franz Hals and a number of other equally famous painters, with Julia displaying a knowledge of these treasures which, it amused her to see, rather surprised her escort. He said at length, 'You know a great deal.'

'Not really,' she answered honestly, 'but when I was a student nurse I hadn't a great deal of money so I spent a lot of time in museums and picture galleries.' They were standing in front of Rembrandt's self-portrait and she smiled at him over her shoulder and surprised a look on his face which set her heart beating a great deal faster than it should. She plunged at once into the first topic of conversation which entered her head, which was, not surprisingly, Rembrandt. She kept up quite a dissertation on him, rivalling her patient in both length and dullness, and only stopped when Ivo said gently,

'It's all right, dear girl—I'm not sure why you took fright, but there is no harm in us recapturing our happy times at Drumlochie House, is there?'

'No,' said Julia instantly, 'but it was easy and natural somehow, wasn't it, to be friends—I suppose it was because we were cut off from everything, in our own world. Now we're normal again and it seems unreal.' She gave him a frank look. 'You're different, too.'

They were walking slowly past priceless paintings which neither of them saw. 'And you are just the same,' said Ivo slowly. 'That's what makes it so hard.' With which cryptic remark she had to be content.

They went up the tower of St Jacobskerk after that, climbing the steps slowly and then standing to admire the view while Ivo pointed out the landmarks around them, recounting old tales and snatches of legends as he did so, so that each one came alive as he spoke. He told her about the village of Haghe, where William the Second had had his hunting lodge, which over the years, had become a town and finally the city it was before them, still keeping its name 'The Hedge'. Only the threatening dusk sent them down at last, to hurry through the streets to Formosa for tea, where they lingered, talking of unimportant things, and Julia, forgetful of everything but the delightful present, was happy.

Only later as they walked down Noordeinde to where Ivo had left his car did she remember, with sudden and painful vividness, Ivo coming out of the jeweller's shop that morning, but she dismissed it instantly and gave herself up to the delightful make-believe world of the present. The future, and Marcia, could be faced when she got back; meanwhile she stopped, obedient to Ivo's hand on her arm, to admire a windowful of toys, and vied with him in picking out which she would have chosen if she had been a child again.

They had only been in the car a minute or so when Jorina joined them, her arms full of parcels and bubbling over with happiness because she had spent the whole afternoon with Klaas.

'He's coming to the party, of course,' she explained to Julia as Ivo threaded his way through the city's heart and out of it through the suburbs. 'He'll stay the night and spend Christmas Day with us—then I shall go back with him to his family in Arnhem.' She drew a breath and went on, 'I found some shoes— brown calf with black patent leather trimming—a little expensive, but just what I wanted.'

She rattled on happily for the rest of the journey home, unnoticing of the other two's silence, but when they were nearly home she asked,

'And what did you two do?'

Julia told her, with occasional comments from Ivo as she did so, making it last as long possible because it was easier to talk than to sit and think. They were all very gay by the time Ivo drew up in front of the house; they went inside together, still laughing and talking, to part in the hall, the girls to go upstairs and Ivo, after taking off his coat, to enter the sitting room, the books he had promised Marcia under his arm.

Julia hardly spoke to him that evening, for after dinner he went to his study and didn't come out until after she had coaxed Marcia up to bed. She went to her own room herself once she had her patient safely between the sheets, for she was tired after her day's sightseeing and even more wearied from Marcia's low-voiced utterances, all of which reiterated her selfless wish to see others enjoying themselves even at the expense of her own comfort and happiness. She had taken care to utter none of these remarks in front of Ivo, though; to him she had been appealingly wistful, interested in their day in the Hague, and while expressing her delight at the success of the outing, managed to convey, without uttering a word to that effect, that both he and Julia had been both selfish and thoughtless.

Julia, brushing her hair with a violence calculated

to tear it out by the roots, remembered Ivo's slight frown as he had listened to Marcia and gave her patient credit for being clever. She got into bed, her mind a prey to a multitude of thoughts, all of them unhappy. She was almost asleep when she remembered that Ivo had kissed her; probably it had meant nothing to him and it had really no right to mean anything to her. All the same, she smiled as she closed her eyes.

CHAPTER SEVEN

THE NEXT DAY was Christmas Eve, and after weeks of bad weather the sun shone from a pale blue sky, giving the frost it wasn't strong enough to disperse an added sprinkle. Julia, going to see how her patient was before breakfast, stopped for a moment to look out of one of the landing windows and admire the wintry scene. It was still not full daylight, although the sun was making a brave blaze of colour on the flat horizon, and somewhere outside she could hear Bep calling to Lien, who came from the village each day to help in the house. Their voices, very clear in the frosty air, sounded cheerful, and that, combined with the sunshine and the aromatic smell of coffee from the kitchen, contrived to put Julia into a cheerful frame of mind; it was, after all, Christmas and a time of good fellowship. She went to Marcia's room, determined to be kind and considerate and even to try and like her patient a little.

It was a pity that Marcia wasn't of the same mind; she greeted Julia with a cross face, a muttered greeting and a rather tart request to hand her a book lying just out of reach. Julia handed it to her, forbearing to mention that she could have quite easily got it for herself, adjusted her patient's pillows to a nicety and went downstairs to see if the post had arrived. It had; she sorted Marcia's scanty mail and went along to the kitchen to get her early morning tea tray, delaying for

154

a few minutes in order to practice her scanty Dutch on Bep before going upstairs. She had deposited the tray, handed over the letters and was on her way to the door when she was stopped.

'Nurse Pennyfeather, I must see Ivo at once—ask him to come to me immediately.' Marcia cast down the letter she had been reading and when Julia didn't move, repeated, 'Do go at once!'

Julia stayed just where she was. She said composedly, 'Ivo's having breakfast—he has to go to Eindhoven this morning. Had you forgotten?'

Miss Jason looked at her through narrowed eyes. 'I don't care if he has to go to Timbuktu,' she pronounced with surprising venom. 'He must come and see me!' She tapped the discarded letter with a nicely manicured hand. 'Did you know that Mijnheer de Winter hasn't received an invitation to the party this evening? After all his kindness to me! I shall refuse to go unless he is invited immediately. Go downstairs and say so, and be quick about it!'

Julia walked slowly back to the bed and stood looking down at the bad-tempered face staring up at her. A pity Ivo couldn't see his Marcia now—Julia suspected that this was neither the first nor the last time her patient had allowed her façade of angelic serenity to slip. She said in a reasonable voice, her own temper nicely under control,

'I don't much care for the way in which you speak to me, Miss Jason. I'm here to look after you, not to be ordered around or expected to run to and fro at your beck and call. You are no longer helpless; you might try to realise that, I think, and behave with more consideration to those around you. If you could remember that we might get on quite well.'

She smiled kindly at the astonished face turned to hers and went without haste from the room.

Ivo was in the hall, putting on his overcoat as she descended the staircase. He gave her the briefest of glances, said, 'Good morning, Julia,' in an absent-minded fashion and made for the door so that she was forced to put on a turn of speed to reach it when he did. She said without preamble, 'Marcia wants to see you urgently—she asks that you should go to her now.'

He paused with his hand on the door. 'Well, I can't—didn't you tell her that I was going to Eind-hoven? Come to think of it, I told her myself yester-day evening.'

'You must,' said Julia firmly, and when he turned a baleful eye upon her: 'It's no good looking at me like that—you didn't invite Mijnheer de Winter, and Miss Jason says that if he doesn't come, she won't either. She's upset.'

She saw his frown as he pushed his briefcase and gloves into her hands and turned and ran up the stairs, two at a time. She stood at the door, trying not to hear the faint murmur of voices from her patient's room, and presently he came down again, his face bleak, took his gloves and case without a word, opened the door and went away. She heard the car tearing down the lane and roar down the road, appar-ently driven by a maniac.

The morning went badly after that. It seemed that Marcia hadn't got her way and as a result she sulked, although when Jorina was around she became merely sadly resigned, which was a great deal worse. However, Julia did her best to take no notice of her patient's ill-humour, but encouraged her to do her exercises in a spirited fashion and when she was asked to turn up the hem of the dress her patient intended wearing to the party, did so, although the time spent on it bit deep into her free afternoon.

The dress was a drab purple, skinnily cut, with a neckline which exposed far too much of Marcia's boniness, but when Julia suggested, with all the tact in the world, that the silk jersey hanging in the wardrobe was one of the prettiest dresses she had seen for a long time, she met with no success.

'I daresay you do like it, nurse,' quoth Miss Jason, 'but with my slender figure I'm able to wear these clinging styles. You, of course, think otherwise, and naturally so, I expect you feel just a teeny bit envious of us willowy creatures. It must be difficult for you big girls to stay in the fashion.'

Julia murmured a nothing in reply; she had a nice taste in clothes and had never considered that fashion had passed her by—indeed, from the admiring glances wolf whistles she collected when out walking, she had always felt that she was as least as eye-catching as the next girl. She thought of the pink wool hanging in her cupboard and took comfort from it.

The party was to be quite a big affair, with a family dinner party at half past seven and the rest of the guests arriving about nine for what Jorina had called a chatty evening with dancing. But Julia, when she peeped into the drawing room, decided that for once Jorina's English hadn't been quite accurate, for the room, a large one, had been cleared for dancing, its magnificent old furniture arranged round its white-painted walls, and the silky carpet rolled up and carried off to some cupboard or other by Bep. There were flowers everywhere, and when Julia put her head round the dining room door, there were flowers there too, and the table, already decked with a lace cloth and a great deal of silver and glass, had a magnificent centre-piece of holly and ivy with Father Christmas, complete with sleigh and reindeer, in the middle.

Jorina came in while Julia was admiring the flowers and said, 'Nice, eh? You like it, I hope. We have twelve for dinner and there will be about fifty people coming afterwards. A nice large party, but this time, bigger than usual, but there is room enough for everyone.'

She moved a bowl of hyacinths from one table to another and asked,

'And Marcia, she feels better now? Does she come to the party after all?' She didn't wait for Julia to answer but went on, 'And why are you not off duty, Julia?'

'I've been altering a dress for Marcia,' said Julia, and choked back a laugh as Jorina exclaimed, 'Not tighter, I hope, or cut lower in the neck—if there are no curves what is the point of letting everyone see?'

She turned round as Bep came into the room with a tray of coffee.

'Now we will sit down and drink our coffee—how fortunate that Marcia feels that she should rest. Was Ivo very angry this morning?'

Julia accepted her cup. 'Very,' she stated simply, remembering his bleak face. They sipped in a comfortable silence, broken by Jorina.

'I wish to talk,' she stated flatly. 'I have wished to talk for many days now. I talk to Vader and he laughs a little and says things have a way of putting themselves right, and I talk to Ivo and that is worse, for although he listens and is polite he is also very angry, so now I talk to you because I think that we are friends.'

Julia heard her with mixed feelings. Jorina was going to talk about Marcia and Ivo. That she didn't like Marcia, Julia was pretty sure, probably she disliked the idea of having her for a sister-in-law... She said a little unhappily, 'Well, I suppose it's all right and I'm glad you think of me as a friend, I like you too, but would Ivo mind?'

'Of course he would mind, but you will not tell and I certainly shall not.' She went on as Julia had expected she would, 'It is about Marcia.' She took Julia's cup and refilled it, then refilled her own. 'You see he doesn't love her—I don't suppose he ever did. Only when they first met she was clever...' Julia gave her a questioning look and she went on quickly, 'I will explain. A long time ago, when Ivo was twenty—twenty-one, he met a girl—she was pretty and—and frivol—how do you say?'

'Frivolous?' essayed Julia. 'Bird-witted?'

Jorina nodded. 'Yes—she led Ivo by the nose, she was so very pretty, you see, and gay and amusing and a little naughty, and then after a few months she married someone else with a great deal of money, and although Ivo has plenty of money too, it was not enough, so for years he had not loved any girl.

'And then last year he meets Marcia at some lecture or other and I think that someone has told her about him because she does not try to flirt or attract him, only she lets him see that she has a good brain and that she reads Greek and Latin and is a very serious person, so he thinks, "Here is a girl who is not after my money or out for a good time", and they become friendly and go to lectures and theatres and concerts—all very dull. Then she is taken ill, and while she is still in hospital Ivo has to go to Edinburgh, and although I am quite sure he has never mentioned marriage to her, she hints and suggests…it is as if she has convinced him that he was responsible for her getting polio—I do not know how.'

'Where did Marcia catch it?' asked Julia quickly.

'At a party to which Ivo took her. She did not wish to go because it was to be gay with dancing, but he persuaded her, and it was after that that she became ill.' She shrugged her shoulders. 'So when she is able to leave hospital she asks that she may come and stay with us until she is strong enough to travel, and because Ivo is not here and we do not know how he feels about her, we agree. But six months is a long time and I think—I know that Ivo does not wish to marry her, but she pretends to him that she loves him very dearly, so he is kind to her, for she is ill and perhaps he thinks that in his absence her feelings will change and everything will arrange itself. But you see how she behaves towards him, Julia; she will marry him, although she does not love him, and I shall not forgive her.'

'Can't you tell her—I mean how Ivo feels?' hazarded Julia. 'No—he wouldn't stand for that, would he? Can't he tell her?'

'Not Ivo. You see, he thinks that she loves him and she pretends—you think that she pretends too?'

'Yes, she doesn't care a row of buttons for him,' said Julia vehemently, and then had to pause to explain about the row of buttons. 'She's in love—as far as she can be—with that awful de Winter man.'

'Then why doesn't she tell Ivo that she doesn't love him?'

Julia thought about this and then said slowly, 'I'm not sure,' although she was almost certain she was. Marcia had been flattered by Ivo's attention—who wouldn't have been? Probably she had decided to marry him within a few weeks of meeting him, but was far too clever to let him see that. When she became ill she had made the most of Ivo's pity and concern for her; possibly she had written him letters calculated to keep that concern alive while he was away—and then August de Winter had come along and in her odd way, she had fallen in love with him, but because she was uncertain of him she had refused to let Ivo go, and now, although she didn't want him any more, she was going to keep up her deception until Julia had returned to England and there was no likelihood of Ivo falling in love with her...because he had fallen in love with her, she wasn't sure how much, and it seemed unlikely that she would ever know. She could of course go to Ivo and tell him about Marcia and August de Winter, and he would despise her for it. She sighed and said, 'Marcia is a very clever woman and there's nothing we can do about it. He'll have to find out for himself and let's hope it won't be too late when he does.'

Jorina surveyed her narrowly, her nice blue eyes

thoughtful. 'Is it not strange,' she said, 'that we are unable to say to each other what we would wish to say? One day, perhaps. What shall we do? I had thought of telling Ivo, but I cannot—I suppose you would not?'

Julia gave her a horrified look. 'Me? Heavens, no! Not for all the tea in China.'

She had to explain that too, she was still doing so when Doctor van den Werff came in and asked with some surprise if they didn't intend to change. 'I know it's still early, but I daresay you'll take a long time, and we shall need a drink before everyone arrives.'

He smiled at them both and went away again and Julia got up to go.

'I don't take long to change, actually, but Marcia will need help.'

Her patient dressed with more eagerness than Julia had expected, and it was while she was zipping the dreary purple up its back that Marcia said coolly, 'I telephoned Mijnheer de Winter while you were downstairs and asked him to come on my own account. Since Ivo disregarded my wishes I was forced to take matters into my own hands.'

Julia fastened the little hook at the top of the zip. 'To dinner?' she asked with admirable calm. 'There are guests, that will make the numbers wrong. And he's not one of the family.'

Miss Jason admired herself in the pier glass. 'Nor are you, nurse,' her voice was spiteful, 'and Ivo should have thought of that—he must learn to have some regard for my wishes.'

Julia tried again. 'But, Miss Jason, it's not your party—you're a guest in the house.'

Marcia turned round to face her, without, Julia noticed mechanically, any difficulty. 'And what business is that of yours? Perhaps you're afraid you'll be asked to dine in your room in order to make the numbers right.' She turned back again and smiled slowly at her reflection. 'This colour suits me—I'll rest now if you want to go.'

Julia went. If she changed very quickly she would have time to go and tell Jorina so that something could be done about dinner. She raced through her bath and was about to put on her dress when she decided to find Jorina at that very moment and not wait any longer. She flung on her dressing gown and with her feet thrust into slippers and her hair streaming blackly down her back, she ran across to Jorina's room, tapped on the door and went in. Jorina was there, also in her dressing gown, and Ivo, still in his dark grey suit, was sitting on the end of her bed.

'Oh, lord,' said Julia helplessly, and turned to go, to be stopped by Ivo's half-laughing: 'Don't run away, Julia—it's not the first time I've seen you in a dressing gown with your hair dripping round your shoulders. What's the matter? Or have you come to borrow something feminine I'm not supposed to know about?'

Julia advanced into the room. 'Look,' she said urgently, 'I wasn't going to tell you, but since you're here—and you'll know soon enough anyway—Marcia has just told me she's invited Mijnheer de Winter to dinner and I feel mean telling you because I'm sure she didn't mean me to.' She ignored Ivo's laugh and went on, 'But you had to know, because that'll make thirteen at table and that would never do—I'll have dinner in my room, it's such a good idea and no one will be any the wiser. Actually I didn't think of it, Marcia did...'

'The devil she did,' said Ivo, and then seriously, 'There's no question of you not coming to dinner,' and she realised then that he was indeed very angry. 'I'll telephone someone—we'll sit down fourteen. There's no need to tell Marcia, for there's no point in arguing about it at this late hour. Thank you for telling us, dear girl—no one need know, just we three, and Bep of course, but she's a tower of silence!' He smiled suddenly and Julia felt her heart slide away into a spiralling pulse. 'Hadn't you better finish dressing, dear Miss Pennyfeather? You look sensational as you are, but no one would eat anything if you appeared at table like that.'

He accompanied her to the door and opened it and as she went past him murmured wickedly, 'If you need any help I'd be delighted.'

She cast him a withering glance and flew down the passage and heard his laugh as she shut her door.

As she dressed it occurred to her that he hadn't been much upset by Marcia's conduct; she had been prepared to be sympathetic, but now it seemed that sympathy was wasted on him.

She put on the new pink dress, piled her hair elegantly and scented her person with 'Femme' before studying herself in the long mirror on the wall. The dress suited her with its high neck and long sleeves and the simplicity of its cut. She went along to Marcia's room to remind her that it was time to join the family downstairs and tried not to notice the inimical look in Marcia's eyes as they lighted upon her. Miss Jason, although ready, was unwilling to go down.

'Kindly go and fetch Ivo,' she said. 'I should like him to help me downstairs.'

It was on the tip of Julia's tongue to tell her that she needed no help, but there was no point in spoiling what she hoped was to be a delightful evening. She went downstairs and had reached the bottom step as Ivo came out of his study. She stammered a little as she spoke to him because he looked handsomer than ever in his dinner jacket, as well as a little remote, but there was nothing remote about his greeting. He walked across the hall towards her and took her hands, held her arms wide and studied her with cool leisure. 'Delightful,' he pronounced, and for a moment she thought that he was going to say something else, but he didn't, so she gave him Marcia's message, standing there, still holding hands, and was a little surprised when he said lightly,

'Ah, yes—this is Marcia's great night, isn't it?'

'Because she's going to dance?'

She didn't understand why he smiled. 'That among other things,' he said in a teasing voice, and led her across the hall to the sitting room where the rest of the dinner party were gathering, and handed her over to his father before he went upstairs, to return very soon with Marcia clinging to his arm. Hard on their heels came August de Winter, looking nervous, and Julia, who disliked him very much, found it in her heart to pity him because of the perfect and icy politeness, with which he was greeted by Ivo and his father; anyone with a thinner skin might have turned tail and left the party on some trumped-up excuse, but he seated himself on a sofa beside Marcia and began a low-voiced conversation with her, while Ivo, looking too bland for Julia's peace of mind, turned to greet the last and fourteenth guest. And no wonder he had looked so bland, she thought, and was thankful that she had wasted no sympathy on him, as he obviously needed none. The girl who came in was small and blonde and very pretty with laughing blue eyes and a gaiety which was infectious. She was wearing the sort of dress most girls long to wear and dared not, and she greeted Ivo with a disturbing familiarity which troubled Julia a little, and the rest of the company with charm, and then, as if drawn by a magnet, fastened like a leech upon Mijnheer de Winter, who was, willy-nilly, prised from Marcia with a neatness which could only earn Julia's wholehearted approbation. She felt almost sorry for the man struggling to withstand the laughing blue eyes of this dolly, against whom he had no chance, and at the same time retain his dignity in Marcia's eyes. He gave up the struggle very soon and was led away, leaving her on the sofa where she was immediately joined by Doctor van den Werff, who, disregarding her discomfiture, broke at once into easy conversation.

Dinner was fun, at least for Julia, who had Ivo's other brother, Pieter, on one side of her and an uncle on the other—the uncle was, as was to be expected, a doctor too. They talked lightheartedly and made her laugh a great deal as they ate their way through oyster soup, filet of beef Meurice and gateau St Honoré, washed down with a variety of wines which certainly contributed, as far as she was concerned, to a delightful meal. It was a leisurely one too; by the time they had all repaired to the drawing room, they were joined almost at once by the first of the guests, and when someone started a CD player, everyone took to the floor. Julia, partnered by yet another cousin who begged her to call him Bill, watched Marcia rise to her feet and circle the room slowly with Ivo, an action made all the more conspicuous because they were doing the foxtrot while everyone else was gyrating in a more up-to-date fashion. Her partner watched them too and observed,

'Is that the young lady who was stricken by polio? A marvellous recovery—in fact she looks as though she's been recovered for some time.'

'Are you a doctor?' asked Julia suspiciously.

He smiled at her charmingly. She thought he was rather nice, not young any more, but possessed of a friendly manner and a pair of twinkling eyes which could, she suspected, be keen as well.

'Yes, my dear young lady; married, with three children, otherwise I would be sitting out with you on the stairs. Has anyone ever told you that you're beautiful?'

'Yes,' said Julia tranquilly, 'they have, but thank you just the same. What made you say that about Miss Jason?'

She was right about the eyes; they became keen on the instant. 'Nothing, my dear, nothing—only it seems to me that she's been here a very long time. In my experience fairly mild cases—fairly severe ones too—respond well to modern treatment and—pull their weight once they are on their feet. I should have thought she would have wanted to go home. Has she no family?'

'Oh, yes—her father's a solicitor in England, some-where in the Midlands.'

He made an amused face. 'I don't like your Mid-lands. I also would not wish to return there. What do you think of Lise?'

'She's the prettiest thing I've seen for weeks,' Julia said sincerely.

They were joined then by more people and almost at once Julia was asked to dance again; this time her partner was young, and although his English wasn't good, they carried on an animated conversation, un-derstanding each other very well, laughing a good deal as they danced. She had a number of partners after that and would doubtless have danced all night if she hadn't caught sight of Marcia, sitting between two great-uncles, and looking discontented. Julia, who had no idea of the time, and didn't really care, deduced that Marcia had had enough of the party; she slipped between the dancers and joined the little group.

'I wondered if you were tired, Miss Jason,' she began, although Miss Jason didn't look tired, only cross which, Julia thought sympathetically, was nat-ural enough, for there was no sign of Ivo and none of August de Winter. 'I thought you danced beauti-fully,' she went on. 'What a triumph after all those months.'

'I fail to see what triumph there is in dancing round a room, Nurse Pennyfeather. I shall go to bed in half an hour, if you could remember I shall be glad of your help.'

'I'll remember,' said Julia, and smiled at the two old gentlemen as she slipped away. If she had only half an hour of the evening left, it would be nice to dance until the last moment of it. She was passing the open door to the hall when Ivo's arm shot out and caught her gently.

'There you are,' he said pleasantly. 'We haven't danced, dear Miss Pennyfeather.' He swung her into the crowd. 'Having a good time?'

'Super. Marcia wants to go to bed in half an hour though, and I shall go up with her. I—I saw her dancing. She was marvellous.'

She looked up at him and he returned her look with a half smile.

'I think August de Winter has enjoyed himself too,' he remarked silkily.

Julia was stricken by a sudden thought. 'Did you do it on purpose, Ivo?'

He made no pretence of not knowing what she meant. 'Of course, dear girl, surely you know by now how disagreeable I can be?' He smiled again, his blue eyes fierce, and then said in quite a different voice,

'Has anyone told you that you look beautiful this evening? You do. I like that demure pink thing—you put every other woman here in the shade, Julia.'

'Who's Lise?' asked Julia, who had been longing to know all the evening.

'Pretty, isn't she? She's theatre sister at Tilburg hospital. Jealous, dear girl?'

Julia went pink. She said much too quickly, 'Of course not, how ridiculous,' and knew that she was, wildly jealous. 'Anyway, why ask me? Is that why you invited her?' she went on, following her own train of thought. She gave him a severe look which he ignored.

'She can't hold a candle to you, Julia. James must be mad to let you out of his sight.'

'Oh, James—pooh,' said Julia impatiently. 'I shan't marry him.'

'No, I know that. Why do you keep looking at the clock?'

She reminded him about Marcia and said hesitantly, 'Would you like to dance with her once more, or—or talk to her before she goes to bed?'

For answer he drew her through the door they were passing. The hall was dimly lighted and empty as they walked over to the fire burning in the steel grate at the back of the hall.

'You're going to miss the rest of the party,' he said kindly. 'Come down again even if everyone has gone. I want to wish you a Happy Christmas before we go to bed.'

They went back together through the babel of laughter and talk and when they reached Marcia, Ivo helped her to her feet and in the little silence which had fallen, said pleasantly, 'I'm sure you're all glad to see what a marvellous recovery Marcia has made. She's going to her room now, but don't think that that signals the end of the evening.'

He smiled, his face calm, but when he would have gone to the door with her, Marcia held back, shaking her head playfully at him in a manner which Julia found quite nauseating. 'You're all so kind,' she said, 'and I am so happy. I should say—we are so happy.' She looked up at Ivo who, Julia was relieved to see, wore a polite, impersonal air of friendliness; if he loved Marcia, then he was hiding it most successfully, and now would have been a wonderful time to have announced his intention to marry—if he was going to marry. With a sudden uplift of spirits she realised that he wasn't going to do anything of the sort, but equally, he wasn't going to humiliate Marcia either. It was the cousin from Utrecht who said exactly the right thing.

'Well, of course we're all happy,' he remarked loudly. 'You're cured, Marcia, which means you're happy because you're the patient, and Ivo's happy because he's the doctor, and we're all happy because you have been able to enjoy the party. Let's drink a toast to that.'

The toast was drunk and Julia, watching Marcia, could see that she was furiously angry.

As she had expected, her patient took a long time to undress, she complained in a low, pained voice as each garment was removed and avowed that permanent damage had been done by reason of the exercise she had been persuaded, against her will, to take. 'I should never have danced,' she stated in the brave, resigned voice she affected when she wished to draw attention to herself. 'But of course, Ivo insisted.'

'There was no reason why you shouldn't,' observed Julia cheerfully, determined to be nice despite her opinion of Marcia's behaviour at the party. 'I know you've been ill a long time, but you're as good as new again, you know. You can't stay an invalid all your life.'

Miss Jason had nothing to say to this, instead she complained once again, this time about the ache in her legs.

'Only your muscles—time they were used a little more,' said Julia reassuringly, but despite her strong feelings, her hands were gentle as, without any show of impatience, she began to massage her patient's legs. By the time she had finished and Marcia had declared herself ready to sleep, they could hear the last of the cars driving away; the guests had gone, the party was over. All the same, Julia, when she found herself free, did as she had promised and went downstairs to a house strangely quiet after the cheerful hubbub of the evening. The fire in the hall was dying down; its heat had brought out the scent of the flowers in a great bowl on one of the console tables and she sniffed appreciatively as she passed it on the way to the drawing room. The drawing room was empty, but when she went into the sitting room it was to find Doctor van den Werff, his three sons, his daughter-in-law and Jorina and Klaas clustered round the fire, a tray of coffee in the middle and the whisky decanter to hand.

Jorina said comfortably, 'We've been talking about the party. Did you enjoy it too?' and when Julia said that she had, very much, they all started talking about it once more, and continued to do so until Doctor van den Werff got up to go to bed, followed, in ones and twos by everyone else, but when Julia went to follow them, Ivo said softly, 'Not you, Julia—stay a few minutes longer.' So she stayed, sitting back comfortably in the deep chair, watching the flickering fire and not talking at all. Ivo had nothing to say either, but it was peaceful there together; somehow there seemed no need for words. But when the clock struck a silvery half hour she roused herself, exclaiming,

'The time! I simply must go to bed,' and was taken aback when Ivo said quietly, 'There is really no need to talk, is there?' and smiled in such a way that she got to her feet rather more hastily than she had intended. 'It was a lovely party,' she gabbled. 'I'll say goodnight,' but Ivo had stood up with her and before she could move away had caught her hands in his.

'It's Christmas Day, Julia—the first day of Christmas.' He let her hands go and fished around in his pocket, to produce a small jeweller's box of red leather and then lift her hand to curl the fingers round it. 'I hope you'll like it, dear Miss Pennyfeather.'

She opened her hand and looked at the box. 'May I open it now?' she asked in a small voice, and taking his silence for consent, lifted the lid. There were earrings inside, resting on white velvet. They were early Victorian, she guessed, small golden crescents ornamented with filigree work in the centre of which was suspended a red stone, set in gold—they looked like rubies, but as it wasn't very likely that Ivo would buy her rubies, she supposed them to be paste, but paste or not, the earrings were very beautiful. She said so in a warm voice and asked if they were Dutch, and when he said briefly, 'Yes,' she went on, 'Thank you, Ivo, what a lovely present. I want to try them on.'

She smiled at him and went across to the baroque mirror on the wall and slipped the delicate little hooks in, swinging her pretty head from side to side to see the effect. She began. 'They're much too...' but was interrupted by his, 'No, they are not, Julia,' and something in his voice prevented her from going on, so she said instead, 'Thank you. Ivo—what a lovely way to start the first day of Christmas.' She smiled at him in the mirror and he said lightly, 'Wear them tomorrow, Julia—think of them as a small return for what you have done for Marcia, if you will.'

'Very well, Ivo. And now I think I'll go to bed. Good night.'

In her room, she took the earrings out of her ears and laid them back in their little box; they had done nothing to discourage her impossible daydreams; it was time she used a little common sense. She got into bed and late though it was, spent some considerable time poring over the time-tables she had purchased in Oisterwijk, so that she could return to England with the least possible fuss, just as soon as Doctor van den Werff suggested she should do so.

She was early for breakfast next morning, but Jorina was already at breakfast with Ivo and her father, although no one else had come down. They greeted her with a cheerful chorus of Merry Christmases and she sat down, to find a small pile of gaily wrapped packages by her plate. She jumped up again at once and said, a little confused, 'Oh, I left mine upstairs— I wasn't quite sure—I'll get them.'

She was back in a minute to give her own small presents before opening her own. Bep's was first—a small Delft blue candlestick, complete with its blue candle. The second was a French silk scarf in coffee patterned with greens and blues, from Jorina, and lastly there was a large square box, which turned out to be marrons glacés, most extravagantly packed and beribboned, from the doctor. She had scarcely finished thanking them when Jorina asked, 'What did Ivo give you?'

Julia glanced at him across the table. He had finished his breakfast and was sitting back in his chair, very relaxed, smiling a little.

'Earrings,' she said simply, 'quite beautiful. Gold crescents with red stones.' She smiled widely, remembering them. 'I shall wear them when I change.'

By the time she was free from her duties, everyone had gone to church. It would have been nice to have gone too, even in a foreign language church would have made the day more Christmassy. She had hoped that Marcia might have expressed a wish to go with the family, but she had protested gently when she had been invited to join them, and Julia had spent the greater part of the morning encouraging her to exercise herself, something she was loath to do.

They all met again at lunchtime, for although Jorina had come upstairs with a request that Marcia and Julia should go down for drinks, Marcia had refused on the grounds that her legs ached. Julia spent half an hour massaging them once more before her patient felt fit for the journey downstairs, and when they eventually reached the sitting room it was to find the men closeted in Ivo's study, enjoying themselves from the sound of things, and Jorina and her sister-in-law sitting together, drinking sherry. They greeted Marcia kindly enough, but their kindliness didn't quite make up for the reception she had expected, for she said in some surprise, 'I had expected everyone to be here...'

Jorina offered her a drink, was refused and said, 'Well, you know what men are—they're in Ivo's study, drinking whisky—they'll be out presently.'

Marcia sat down, took the various packages from Julia which she had been bidden to carry downstairs, and said, 'Well, in that case…' and handed Jorina her gift with a flowery speech which its contents hardly merited. Julia, eyeing it, decided she could have well done without it, had it been offered to her; perhaps she had been lucky in the bookmark after all, for Jorina was staring nonplussed as *The Seven Types of Ambiguity* and quite obviously searching for the right words with which to express her thanks.

The other men came in then and Marcia gave first doctor and then Ivo their gifts and then accepted theirs with a girlish flutter which caused Julia to get up and walk over to the window, from where she watched the doctor unwrap a diary which he exclaimed over politely, tactfully omitting to mention that he received several of exactly the same pattern, free each Christmas, from the various pharmaceutical firms enjoying his patronage. Ivo thanked her gravely too his face blandly polite as he exhibited a tie, a floral one very gay and aggressively nylon—and he, Julia was certain, wore nothing but pure silk, handmade, and those in dark rich colours. And for Bep, Marcia had nothing at all, which didn't worry her in the least, for after her own careless, 'Oh, her—I'd forgotten,' she undid her own presents. And very dull too, thought Julia while her patient exclaimed rapturously over a Greek-English dictionary which the doctor had thoughtfully given her and a beautifully bound volume of Montaigne's Essays from Ivo—not a very loving gift, thought Julia, and felt a guilty delight in her earrings.

Lunch, a light meal, because they were going to dine traditionally that evening, passed off smoothly enough, and Julia, watching Ivo discreetly through her long lashes, could see nothing in his pleasant friendly manner towards Marcia to suggest that he was in love with her, although she was shrewd enough to realise that he wasn't a man to show his feelings in public—at least, she amended, only if his feelings got the better of him, and those, she considered, he had nicely under control. It was a pity she could tell nothing from his face. He was looking at her now and she hadn't heard a word he said.

'Daydreaming,' he remarked. 'I'll have to say it all again. What are you going to do this afternoon?'

'Go for a walk,' she replied promptly, because it was the first thing to enter her head.

'I'll come with you if I may,' he said easily. 'I could do with some exercise.'

Without looking at her Julia knew that Marcia was annoyed, although when she spoke, that young woman's voice was as well modulated as always, although faintly long-suffering.

'Ivo,' she said, 'I had hoped that we might have had a pleasant afternoon—do you know, we've hardly talked since you have been back?'

'Indeed?' Ivo was at his silkiest, but perhaps it was because he was still annoyed about August de Winter and wanted to teach her a lesson. Julia frowned; she didn't care be used for his convenience—she wouldn't go for a walk...

'This evening, perhaps,' Ivo went on vaguely with a pleasant smile. 'Shouldn't you rest now?' He glanced across at Jorina. 'We're dining early, aren't we, Jorina—?' and when she nodded continued to Marcia, 'There are a few friends coming in this evening, you don't want to be too tired.'

They got up from the table and as they did so he said to Julia,

'Hadn't you better hurry up and change, or we shall have no time for our walk,' and because there seemed to be a little pause in the talk as he spoke, Julia said meekly that yes, she would go right away.

It was barely a quarter of an hour later when she came flying down the stairs again, warmly wrapped against the cold, the fur bonnet tied securely under her chin, her feet snug in high leather boots. She pulled on her gloves as she reached the last stair and looked around for Ivo. He was lounging in his study doorway, watching her, and as she exclaimed, 'Oh, there you are,' crossed the hall to meet her, exclaiming,

'You look so happy, dear girl. Why is that?'

She was happy, but it was impossible to tell him that it was because she was going to spend the afternoon with him. 'It's Christmas,' she stated, as though that explained everything.

They started off briskly, for although, for once, the sun was shining and the sky was almost clear of clouds, there had been a heavy frost during the night and it was cold.

They walked in silence, and Julia, trying to think of something ambiguous that would hold no pitfalls conversationwise, asked, 'Was the church full?'

He tucked a hand beneath her elbow. 'Yes, very. I wish you could have been there. I had hoped that you might be.'

'So did I, but I couldn't have left Marcia. She was tired after the party—it was wonderful to see her dancing.'

His hand tightened and she winced from the pain. 'Don't let's talk about her, not now, Julia. Let's pretend we're back at Drumlochie House.'

On the way back Julia asked, 'How many people are coming tonight, Ivo?'

'Oh, a dozen or so—mostly neighbouring doctors and friends from the hospitals—they don't stay late. I'm afraid it's a splendid chance for us to talk shop. Jorina will be glad to have you there to break us up when we get too engrossed.'

'Jorina's a dear,' said Julia with conviction. 'She'll be a wonderful wife. Klaas is a lucky man.'

Ivo stopped to stare down at her. 'And whoever gets you for a wife will be a lucky man too, Julia.'

Her heart sank a little; it seemed as though he took it for granted that she would marry; someone in England, in the future neither of them knew anything about. She told herself she was being foolish and said too brightly, 'Oh, no, he won't. I don't think I'm very good with money and I love pretty clothes and I'm not in the least clever.'

'You sound ideal,' said Ivo, and put up a hand and pushed her bonnet to the back of her head so that her black hair spilled out. He pushed that aside too, gently. 'You're wearing the earrings,' he said, and smiled a little.

'Of course. Aren't they lovely?' she wanted to know, and went pink when he said, 'Almost as lovely as you, Julia.'

He bent and kissed her gently and said, as he had said before, 'Only a seasonal greeting,' and then tucked her hair back inside the bonnet and pulled it forward. And Julia, shaken by his quiet, serious face, said, as she too had said, 'Yes—well, shouldn't we be going back?'

That night, lying in bed with the house quiet around her and only the wind in the trees outside to disturb her thoughts, Julia tried to make plans again, but it was of no use and she allowed her thoughts to drift instead to the pleasant evening they had all enjoyed. For it had been that; they had dined off roast turkey with its attendant chestnut stuffing and cranberry sauce and what Jorina described as English vegetables culled from an old copy of Mrs Beeton's cookery book. There was even a Christmas pudding, and Julia had found it rather touching that Jorina had gone to such pains to have everything just right. They had finished with crackers to pull and the champagne which Ivo had produced had loosened their tongues to a gaiety which even Marcia joined in.

Later, when the guests had arrived, it had been fun too; they had teased her in their beautiful English about the few words of Dutch she managed to say and she had laughed with them, not in the least put out, and even contrived to add to her vocabulary. Somehow Ivo had been beside her for the greater part of the evening, and when everyone had gone and she was waiting at the foot of the stairs while Marcia said her goodnights, he had come to her and asked her if she had had a happy day. She had nodded, her eyes alight with happiness, the earrings dancing, and had longed to ask him if he had been happy too—and didn't dare for fear of the answer. So she had smiled at him, saying nothing, her vivid face aglow, forgetful of her feelings, and then turned to see Marcia watching them from the drawing room door.

She hadn't been surprised when Marcia, as she was getting ready for bed, asked her who had given her the earrings; she had been able to answer naturally enough that it was Ivo. 'Something to remind me of Holland when I go back,' she said lightly, and Marcia had said nothing to that, nor had she made answer when presently Julia wished her goodnight.

In her own room she had taken the earrings off and laid them carefully away in their little box. She didn't think she would wear them for a long time, not until she could bear to think of Ivo without wanting to burst into tears—something which she immediately did.

CHAPTER EIGHT

JULIA, SLEEPING HEAVILY after a wakeful night, was roused by Jorina's knock early the next morning. She was already dressed in her outdoor things and said happily,

'Klaas and I are just off. The others have just gone—I know it's early, but I wanted to say goodbye, as I shan't be back for a day or two. There's the date to fix for the wedding and several things to decide about the flat, and Klaas is free until the twenty-eighth.'

She sat down on the end of the bed and looked closely at Julia.

'You look—have you been crying? I do believe you have. Has Ivo been beastly to you? He can be a perfect fiend if he loses his temper. The trouble is, it's hard to tell when he does, because he goes all remote.'

Julia shook her head. 'No, it's not Ivo.' Perhaps it would have been better if he had been remote and stayed that way, then she could have nurtured a dislike of him.

'Oh—it's Marcia, is it? I expect she took exception to the earrings—they're rather nice, aren't they? I like rubies.' Jorina ignored Julia's open mouth and went on smoothly, 'It's her own fault. I mean, if you're fool enough to despise such things, you deserve to get dry-as-dust books, don't you? You know, Julia,

I'm beginning to wonder if she will ever go back to England. I asked Ivo and he looked like a thunder-cloud and told me to keep my nose out of his business—there's a brother for you! But all that awful coyness at the party—I mean, anyone listening to her might have thought...it's going to make it much harder for him.'

'Why?' asked Julia, trying to look disinterested.

'Well, as long as he thought Marcia was really in love with him I believe he would have gone to any length not to hurt her, but now he knows about Au-gust de Winter, he'll wait his chance to—to disengage himself without making her look a fool—though I wouldn't be so nice about it, I can tell you. Only I hope she'll give him the chance.'

She jumped up, exclaiming, 'Well, have a pleasant time. It's the second day of Christmas, after all, though I don't think we're quite as merry about it as you are in England with your Boxing Day.'

She smiled and nodded and was gone, and a minute or two later Julia heard the car leaving the house. She got up then, for Christmas or no Christmas, Marcia needed to be coaxed through her exercises and helped in a dozen small ways.

She was a little late for breakfast because Marcia had awakened a little grumpy and was ready to find fault with everything, and Julia, reminding herself that perhaps her patient didn't feel as well as usual, was patient and calm and good-natured with her until at length Marcia pronounced herself satisfied.

Father and son were already at table as she entered the dining room, between them they sat her down, rang for fresh coffee and offered her the bread basket, and although they both gave her similar searching glances neither of them commented upon her pale cheeks, but wished her a good morning and reminded her they would be going to Utrecht in the afternoon.

The morning passed slowly, the more so because there was no sign of Ivo when they went downstairs, only his father and a handful of friends who had called in to wish them the compliments of the season, and drink their health in the doctor's excellent sherry. They chatted politely to the two girls, their nice manners standing them in good stead when Marcia rather patronisingly complimented them on their English. One of them, who Julia knew was a professor of surgery at Breda hospital with an English degree as well as several Dutch ones, wanted to know what Marcia thought of his own language, 'For,' said he, 'of course you will have learned to speak it while you have been with us all these months, Miss Jason.' He had smiled blandly at her and when she had confessed that she knew no Dutch at all he turned to Julia and asked,

'And you, young lady—you have been with us long enough to be able to say *ja* or *neen*, have you not?'

Julia gave him the benefit of her nicest smile and said, '*Ja*, Professor,' and went on to recite her meagre, badly pronounced vocabulary, and when she had finished everyone cried 'Bravo!' and raised their glasses, declaring that she had made a very good start, to which she cheerfully agreed, joining in their laughter, and while she laughed suddenly wondered where Ivo was, for he should most certainly have been there. She looked round carefully to make sure she hadn't missed him and caught the doctor's eye; she blushed when he walked across the room to her and asked quietly, 'Looking for Ivo, are you not? He went out to see a child—he shouldn't be long.'

But he was; they waited lunch for half an hour, and when he still hadn't come home, the three of them sat down to cold turkey and salad and a rich pudding of Bep's own make. They had almost finished when he joined them with a murmured word of apology and started his own lunch while they stayed at the table, drinking their coffee and keeping him company, entertaining him with an account of their visitors that morning.

Ivo obviously had something on his mind; he would tell his father after lunch, but in the meantime there seemed no reason for them all to sit in gloom. The conversation, such as it was, was sustained until Ivo began on his coffee, when Julia said,

'Miss Jason, shall we go to the sitting room? I'm sure the doctors want to talk shop, and they wouldn't want to bore us.' Which wasn't quite true. Julia for one was dying to know what could have happened to make Ivo look so serious. She pushed back her chair and hoped Marcia would do the same, but even as she did so, Ivo said, 'No, Julia, don't go,' and turned to Marcia. 'I must ask you to do without Julia for a day or two, Marcia—I need her help for an emergency in Oisterwijk.'

Julia sat very still, watching him; he hadn't bothered to ask her if she wanted or was willing to help. She reflected that sometimes it was nice to be taken for granted in such matters and wondered what the emergency might be. As did Marcia.

'Unless it's very urgent, I don't see how you can

ask that of me,' she said. She gave him a melting look and pouted, 'I need such a lot of care, Ivo.'

Julia bit back her explosive opinion of this remark and waited to hear what Ivo would say.

'It is urgent—there's a case of polio in Biezel. It's only a small village, but a lot of the children who live there come into Oisterwijk to school. There are two other cases I'm not quite certain about. I've done lumbar punctures and sent them in to the path lab in Tilburg, but we can't get a result in under two days. I think we should do a mass inoculation—that's why I want Julia.'

Julia took this piece of news calmly; emergencies cropped up frequently in her working life and she had learnt not to get flustered. But Marcia was more than flustered. She exclaimed in a voice shrill with feeling, 'Polio—and you dare to sit down to table with us, Ivo! It's criminal, we may all become infected!'

He gave her a slow thoughtful look and said with patient courtesy,

'I'm neither criminal nor negligent, Marcia. You yourself are quite immune, and we three have at some time or other in our lives been immunized.'

'I still think it's running unnecessary risks to my health. You can't take Nurse Pennyfeather from me. I'm quite unable to look after myself, and I refuse to be looked after by someone who has become open to infection.'

Julia, watching Ivo, knew now what Jorina had meant when she had told her that Ivo became remote when he was angry. He seemed a different man, although his expression was still pleasant enough as he said patiently,

'You are perfectly able to look after yourself now, Marcia. From your letters, you know, I had the impression that you had made little or no progress, but that is not so, is it? You are well, or almost so. A day or so without Julia to fetch and carry for you will give you all the stimulus you need.'

Julia inquired, 'The child—how old is he?'

Ivo smiled at her and passed his cup for more coffee. 'It's a she—twelve years old and unfortunately goes to school in Oisterwijk. She went to a children's party there on Christmas Eve, too. Her mother told me that she didn't feel well when she went but insisted on going.'

'She's very ill?'

He nodded. 'Yes—all the classic symptoms, and paralysis has set in. I got her into hospital. I must go back and have a look at the other two.'

Marcia spoke and they both turned to look at her, a little guilty because they had quite forgotten she was there. 'What about me?' she wanted to know. 'What am I supposed to do all alone here—what about the dinner party this evening?'

'No dinner party, I'm afraid,' said Ivo in what Julia considered to be far too careless a tone. 'If we mean to do a mass immunisation, we shall need to get organised, and that will take the rest of the day. We'll have to get hold of the school health authorities and find out which children have been immunised, for a start. They'll come first, then the contacts—everyone, in fact.'

'Oisterwijk too?' asked Julia. Her mind boggled at the thought of all the odd Dutch names to be written

on to the official forms someone was bound to produce.

Ivo nodded; as though he had read her thoughts he
said,

'It won't be too bad. We've our own medical rec-
ords and almost everyone in the area is a patient of
one or other of us. If we have to do the lot I'll find
someone to do the writing. You'll be of more use to
us with a swab and a syringe in your hand.'

Julia looked relieved. 'What's to be done first?'

'The practical Nurse Pennyfeather!' He looked, just
for a moment, almost gay. 'If, when you've made sure
Marcia has all she wants in the sitting room, you
would come to my study—we'll check through the
cards of the children who were at the party and make
sure they have all been immunized. That at least we
can do.' And in answer to her look of inquiry, 'Yes,
I remembered to get a list of the children who were
there—that's what you wanted to know, wasn't it?'

Long before they were finished there were two
more calls to children who had been taken ill. Julia
went with Ivo and laid out the lumbar puncture set
while he examined them, and then, masked and
gowned, held them in a neat curve while he did it.
He worked quickly and accurately and with complete
relaxation, and he was kind to the parents as well as
his little patients, who, sadly enough, were very ill.
Ivo arranged for them to go to hospital, then set about
inoculating everyone who had been in contact with
the children during the last few days.

When they returned from the second case it was to
find that Doctor van den Werff had contacted the
health authorities and arranged for supplies of vaccine

as well as syringes and needles to be delivered—he had notified the police too and arranged to take over the school houses in Beizel and Oisterwijk. 'I said we'd start at seven tomorrow morning,' he explained calmly.

Julia felt a little guilty about Marcia, left alone all the afternoon, and expected her to be sulky and difficult, so she was completely knocked off balance by that young lady's manner. It was a mixture of sweet sympathy and eagerness to hear about their activities, allied with subtle turning of the tables against Julia, which happily the men didn't seem to notice.

Julia stole a look at Ivo and saw the little furrow between his brows again, and when she got up to go on some errand for the doctor, he gave her a look which chilled her with its bleakness. Presently he followed her to make sure that she had packed everything they would need for the morning and his manner, although friendly, was remote, as though he were deep in thought and had no time for her. Jorina had said that he would never hurt Marcia, and Julia was beginning to think that she was right, especially as he felt responsible for her illness... They finished at length, and only as she was leaving the surgery did he look directly at her and say quietly. 'Thanks, Julia,' and then, 'You don't understand, do you?'

And she, knowing perfectly well what he meant, paused at the door to reply, 'Yes, I do, Ivo. I expect if I were you I should do the same as you intend to do,' and was surprised to see his face suddenly crease into a smile. 'No, you wouldn't, Miss Pennyfeather, you're much too nice, but thank you for your good opinion even though it's sadly inaccurate.'

It was still very dark when she got up the next morning; she had seen Bep the night before about Marcia's breakfast and any help she might need during the day, so all she had to do was to drink her coffee and eat the toast provided for her. Both men had already breakfasted, they informed her as they left her at table, with the warning that they would be at the front door in ten minutes.

It had been arranged that Ivo, with Julia to help him, should hold the clinic in the schoolhouse in Oisterwijk and that his father, with the help of a borrowed nurse from Tilburg, should take the smaller one in Beizel which, they hoped, would be finished in a day, leaving them free to join Ivo, together with a team of doctors and nurses from the hospital. The whole operation, allowing for setbacks and the absence of the doctors from time to time, should be completed in three days. They had been assured of the fullest co-operation from the Health Department and if they found themselves snowed under they could always ask for help, although, over the holidays, the staff problem was difficult.

They left the house together, Doctor van den Werff driving himself in the Mercedes, and Julia sitting beside Ivo in the Jensen.

There was already a group of people outside the school when they arrived. From somewhere or other Ivo had conjured up two clerical helpers who proceeded to sit themselves at two desks, the cards piled before them. They looked like housewives, not very young but pleasant and calm. Ivo, taking off his coat and hanging it with Julia's on a peg behind the door of the classroom they were using, introduced them as

Mevrouw Cats and Mevrouw van Bek, and hardly giving the ladies time to do more than smile at each other, said, 'Julia, I shall want you to draw up the injections and swab the arms, right?' He glanced at her. 'If I have to go away, you must carry on. Don't bother about anything else, just keep on with the jabs.' He smiled at her briefly and said, 'Right—let's get started.'

It seemed to Julia that the queue snaking slowly past Mevrouw Cats and Mevrouw van Bek never diminished. Even working fast—and Ivo, she discovered, worked very fast—they seemed to make no impression upon it whatsoever. At first it was the young mothers with babies—the babies, unaware of what was happening, remained happy enough, sucking down the three drops of vaccine, nicely flavoured, before their mothers rolled up their sleeves ready for Ivo's needle. But presently the babies petered out a little and the toddlers—those who, for some reason or other, had never been immunised—arrived. Not liking the idea at all, they fought, screaming at the tops of their powerful little lungs while they were divested of their outer garments, resisting at every button and every zip and sliding with the smooth slipperiness of cooked macaroni in and out of their mothers' grasps until caught and held firmly in Julia's lap as Ivo slid the needle in.

The older children were a little easier, although there seemed a great many of them; but they were beginning to make an impression on the piles of cards at last, or so it seemed until Ivo went away. A young woman had come running in as he was about to inoculate a small girl's arm and disregarding everyone around her, had burst into speech. Ivo finished with the little girl, pulled her blonde pigtail gently and got up. 'There's another child,' he said. 'Just keep things going until I get back, will you, dear girl?'

Julia, already piling syringes, needles, swabs and spirit bottle handily, nodded. 'I hope it's not bad,' she said briefly, and gave him a little smile as she turned to the next patient, then remembered to say over her shoulder, 'Leave the address—just in case.'

She was glad of that half an hour later when a man came pushing through the waiting queue and addressed her urgently. She waited until he had finished and then asked 'Doctor?' and when he nodded, copied the address Ivo had left and gave it to the man, glancing at the clock as she did so. It was already gone eleven o'clock and the queue had doubled in size.

It was almost half past one when Ivo finally appeared, to take off his overcoat, put on his white coat and mask again and pick up the syringe Julia was holding ready. He plunged the needle in, grinned at the small boy who was getting it and said,

'Nice work, Julia—sorry you've been on your own.' He looked round the room, his quiet eyes missing nothing. 'A good crowd still—the more the better.'

Julia swabbed the arm before her. 'You got the second message?'

'Yes—I sent the first child to hospital. This one isn't too bad, but he's gone too, of course. Now get that gown off and go across the road to the hotel. Ask for coffee and sandwiches and sit down and eat them—I'll pay later on. You can have fifteen minutes. When you come back I'll go.'

They hardly spoke again, only when it had something to do with their work, and although she was beginning to get tired, Julia would have liked the afternoon to last for ever because Ivo was there with her, but four o'clock came and a relief medical team with it, and with barely a pause in the work, they took over, and Julia found herself outside in the tree-lined main street of the little town, being urged towards the Jensen.

'I'll run you home first,' said Ivo, 'before I start my visits.'

She got in beside him. 'No—there's no need, and it would be a dreadful waste of time—I'm quite happy sitting in the car.'

He gave her a grateful look. 'Accommodating girl,' he said lightly, 'there aren't very many. You can go to sleep if you like.'

But she didn't go to sleep, she thought, and as he was speeding home after his final visit she asked tentatively, 'Doesn't Jorina usually help you with the surgery when it's a big one?'

'Yes—why?'

'Well, wouldn't I do instead? I believe I could manage. I've been thinking about it—and it would save you and your father some time if I sent the people in when you ring...'

He swung the car into the little lane and stopped unfussily exactly in front of the door. 'Clever Julia,' he said with kindly mockery. 'Why not? It'll certainly help, but what about language?'

'Well, I shan't need to say much, shall I? I'll manage, and if I get stuck I'll come to you for help.'

They got out of the car. 'You're not too tired?' he

asked, and she said at once, 'No more than you or Doctor van den Werff are.' They went into the house then, to be met by Bep with the welcome news that she had tea waiting for them.

'I'll put on another uniform first,' said Julia, and disappeared to her room. When she came down ten minutes later, Ivo was in the sitting room with Marcia, who, Julia immediately observed, was being gentle and understanding and very much the brave little woman again. She paused in her talk with Ivo just long enough to give Julia a brief smile which held triumph and complacency, letting her see how easy it was to get a man's attention, even if she weren't a black-haired beauty who knew all about germs and cultures and how to bake bread. And Julia, always a girl to accept a challenge, smiled back, ignoring Ivo and applying herself to her tea, while she listened to the intelligent questions Marcia was putting to Ivo. The girl was really very clever, but she wasn't, it seemed, to have it all her own way, for when Doctor van den Werff came in a few minutes later, he took the conversation in the politest way imaginable into his own hands, and, almost as though he had been listening at the door, proceeded to praise Julia in glowing terms for her part in the day's work; something which she found embarrassing, for she had, before this, worked far harder on a hospital ward, where it had been taken for granted and gone unthanked. She was about to remark on this when she caught the doctor's eye upon her; he was smiling and looked so very like Ivo that she smiled back with a warmth of which she was quite unaware. A moment later he had half-closed his eyes, leaving her to wonder what he had been thinking. But he had most effectively broken up the conversation Marcia had started with Ivo, and it cheered Julia a little to see how quickly Ivo left her side with some light excuse and went to sit by his father, discussing their plans for the next day.

Presently they got up and went away to Ivo's study, and presently, too, it was six o'clock, and to her relief she went to usher the first of the patients into the waiting room at the side of the house.

They finished just before eight o'clock and went in to a late dinner—a meal at which Marcia shone both in appearance and conversation, for Julia was by now too tired to do more than push her cap straight on her rather untidy hair and scrub her capable little hands for the hundredth time that day. Nor did she contribute much to the talk, leaving it to Marcia to continue in her role of sympathetic listener and interested questioner. She had looked up once or twice during the meal to find Ivo's eyes upon her, but beyond a half smile and an odd word, he hadn't addressed her directly except to invite her agreement or opinion upon some point touching their work.

They hadn't been in the sitting room for more than half an hour before Ivo suggested that as they would be starting at seven the next morning, she might like to go to bed, and when she had hesitated he said easily, 'Bep can take Marcia upstairs if she needs help, but I don't imagine she does. In any case, did you not say that you didn't require Julia's services any more, Marcia?' His voice was smooth, though he was smiling, and Marcia's long face became wary.

'I'm sure Nurse is anxious to get back to England,'

she said in the gentle voice Julia so disliked, 'but I suppose she will stay until your little crisis is over.'

Ivo answered her a little coldly, 'If you mean by "little crisis" the risk of a great number of people—mostly young—suffering from the same illness which you have yourself had and from which you have so successfully recovered—yes.'

Which remark, uttered in a silky voice, got Julia to her feet, because probably they intended to discuss her departure and she had very little energy to contribute to the discussion, even if they invited her to do so. She said goodnight rather abruptly and went up to bed, and lay awake until two o'clock in the morning, telling herself, each time she turned over her pillow and rearranged the bedclothes, that as far as she was concerned, the sooner she went home the better.

In consequence the next morning she presented a pale face at breakfast, and when Ivo asked her kindly if she would rather not go with him to Oisterwijk, she snapped, 'Of course I shall come—why do you ask?' and frowned so forbiddingly that he said mildly, 'well, don't slay me, Julia. I only wondered if you felt too tired.'

She poured a second cup of coffee. 'I'm not in the least tired,' she informed him haughtily, and was even crosser when he said carelessly,

'Oh, good, just bad-tempered.'

The desire to say something telling concerning those who worked and those who sat at home doing nothing, while quite unfair, was nevertheless very great. Against her better judgment she had her mouth open to utter something along these lines when Doctor van den Werff forestalled her by remarking smoothly that as she had been such a great help on the previous evening he hoped that she would be prepared to lend a hand that evening as well. 'I shall be finished at Beizel by midday,' he went on, 'so Nurse and I will join you two and the team coming out from Tilburg. We should finish some time tomorrow.'

He gave her a smile of great charm and turned to Ivo. 'We should get the results of the culture by midday,' he observed. 'I hope we caught it in time... thank God most of the babies had been at least partly immunised.'

The conversation was on safe ground once more and stayed so for the remainder of the meal and during the short drive to the schoolhouse, although Julia, for her part, remained a little cold. He had, after all, accused her of being bad-tempered.

The day went much the same as the previous one had, although now that there were more doctors and nurses they got through many more patients. But they still kept on coming; not only from Oisterwijk itself but from the outlying farms and smallholdings and hamlets tucked away in the heath surrounding the little town.

Between twelve and two o'clock they went, team by team, to eat a quick lunch, and Julia, whose temper was quite restored, found herself looking forward to half an hour in Ivo's company; she was of course in his company now, and had been all the morning, but working together was not the same as just being together; they had exchanged barely half a dozen words and those concerned their work. It was a pity that just as they were leaving the schoolhouse, someone should come after them with a message that Ivo was wanted on the telephone. She crossed the street alone and went into the coffee room, where she ordered their coffee and ham rolls and sat down to wait—half an hour wasn't long and five minutes of it had gone already. Ivo came shortly after, though; there was still twenty minutes of time—away from work perhaps she could steer the conversation round to the vexed question of when she was to leave. It was like turning the knife in a wound to bring it up, but Marcia had mentioned it twice already; had in fact disclaimed her need for a nurse any longer. She was only still with them because they needed another pair of hands.

Her carefully laid plans were wasted; all Ivo talked about were the results of the CSF cultures—the first one was through and it was positive, as everyone had expected it would be. She listened to him speculating as to how many more cases they might expect, nodding agreement to his quick-thinking statistics as though she had worked them out for herself, whereas she wasn't actually listening at all.

'Wasted breath,' said Ivo suddenly, and she pinkened under his quizzical look. She said, 'Yes—no, that is, it's very interesting. Ivo, I want to ask you, when am I...' to be interrupted by his brisk, 'Time we went back, come along.'

He got to his feet and paid the bill, then accompanied her back to the schoolhouse, where they were once more plunged in work and spoke hardly a word to each other until four o'clock when their relief arrived.

Julia had hoped to talk to him again on the way home; there would be time between his visits, but today he didn't give her the opportunity to go with him but drove her straight back to the house, set her down at the door, said that he would be back in an hour or so and tore off down the lane again.

She felt better when she had bathed and put on another uniform. She did her face and hair carefully and dabbed a little Chanel Number Five here and there; it might not be quite the thing for a girl in uniform, but it gave her a badly needed uplift, and she might need that because Marcia would be the only one in the sitting room and Marcia wanted her out of the way. She went slowly downstairs and slowed to a halt half-way down, because the sitting room door had opened and Marcia and August de Winter were standing together silhouetted against the soft glow of the room's lamps. Julia watched them as they kissed, too surprised to move, and went on watching as Mijnheer de Winter crossed the hall and let himself out into the evening, while Marcia went back into the sitting room and shut the door gently. Only then did Julia continue on her way, wondering if what she had just seen had been actual fact or just her tired imagination. She stood for a few moments in the hall, listening for a car, but there was no sound; Mijnheer de Winter had either walked or parked his car somewhere along the road. She opened the sitting room door and went in. Marcia was draped on one of the sofas, languidly turning the pages of some tome or other, but she looked up as Julia went in and said, 'Oh, there you are. Well, at least you're someone—I have been lonely all day by myself.'

'And that,' said Julia vulgarly and in a towering rage, 'is a load of old trot! I've just this minute seen you and Mijnheer de Winter kissing each other good-bye. Has he been here all day? I suppose that just because Ivo said he would do his visits after the clinic, you banked on me being with him and not coming home until five or thereabouts. Well, I came home at four!' She crossed the room and stood in front of Marcia, glowing with indignation. 'You seem to think that the whole lot of us are blind and deaf to your goings-on. Well, I for one am not! It's sickening the way you bleat to Ivo about your loneliness and self-sacrifice and bravery each time you see him, while all the time you're none of these things.'

Julia drew a deep breath, looking quite magnificent. 'You are,' she said clearly and unhurriedly, 'a complete fraud. I knew it the moment I set eyes on you—Oh, you had polio, but not as badly as you would have everyone believe, and you've recovered from it weeks ago. I suppose when you came here to stay you had made up your mind to marry Ivo—you bamboozled him into feeling responsible for you getting polio in the first place, didn't you, because he persuaded you to go to a party where there was someone already infected—but I doubt if that was ever proved. I expect you put the idea into everyone's head and no one thought to disbelieve you. Well, I disbelieve you, Marcia. And then you met August de Winter, but you had to go on pretending you loved Ivo, didn't you, so that you could stay here and you could see your August as often as possible while he made up his mind.' She stared down at Marcia, her dark eyes flashing with her wrath. 'You're a harpy,' she said deliberately, 'and a complete fraud!' Then she sat down and waited to hear what Marcia would say.

For once Marcia found words difficult to come by and when she did speak her low measured voice had become almost strident.

'How dare you—' she began, and then with a vicious little smile, 'You're in love with Ivo, aren't you? I know that—that's why I said I didn't want you any more. I don't want him, not now, but I'll take good care that you don't get him. Don't think you'll get away with anything, dear, dear Julia, for you won't. What I intend to do is my own business, but you'll know soon enough...' She broke off as Bep came in with the tea tray, murmuring, *''N beetje laat,'* as she set it down by Julia, and Julia wondered if she and Marcia would have stayed silent for ever and ever if Bep hadn't been late.

They drank their tea in silence and when they had finished Marcia went back to her book, just as though Julia wasn't there, while Julia picked up *Elsevier's Weekblad* and turned to the small ads page, because by reading the columns of bedsitters to let and help in the house wanted, she had picked up several useful words. They were still sitting, the picture of silent companionship, when Doctor van den Werff came in an hour later. He left again after a few pleasantries, pleading work in his surgery, and was followed shortly after by Ivo, who came in, sat down and drank the cup of coffee Bep insisted that he should have, talking idly as he did so, before getting up in his turn. He was halfway to the door when Marcia said with gentle firmness, 'Ivo, I want to talk to you—could you manage a few minutes some time this evening?'

He stood with his hand on the door and said with his usual courtesy, 'Why, of course, Marcia. After surgery, I should think—no, we had better say after dinner. We can be comfortable in my study.' He glanced at the great Zaandse clock on the wall. 'I must go now, though—surgery starts in ten minutes and I've some telephone calls to make first.'

He left the room and a few minutes later Julia got up and went out of the room too to admit the first patient. Neither Marcia nor Julia looked at each other as she went, nor did they speak.

The surgery went well, although it was packed out. Halfway through it Julia slipped into Doctor van den Werff's surgery and asked,

'Shall I ask Bep to delay supper?—the waiting room's still full.'

He looked up from the notes he was reading. 'Do that, Julia. How many patients are there still to see?'

'Four for Ivo, six for you.'

'I wonder if they're quick ones?' He started to shuffle through the patients' cards before him in a rather untidy fashion. Julia took them away from him, restored them to order and said,

'An old man with ear muffs and a Vandyck beard is the next—he's deaf, then a mother with a baby who's got the earache; a girl who looks as though she's going to have twins within the hour, a woman with a black eye, and a fierce old lady with a very small boy who's got a nasty cold.'

Dr van den Werff sat back in his chair and laughed. 'My dear Julia, how very observant you are—shall we tell Bep forty minutes or so?'

She nodded and went to the door and his voice, so very like his son's followed, 'Am I right in thinking that you and Marcia have—er—fallen out?'

Julia turned to face him. 'Yes, we've quarrelled. How did you know?'

'You must give Ivo the credit for that. He's perceptive. He's also very deep; perhaps you didn't know that?'

Julia said carefully, 'It doesn't really matter if I know or not, does it?' and went out, shutting the door carefully behind her.

They sat down to a late dinner presently, and to a conversation which, while easy enough on the part of the two men, sounded decidedly false when the ladies took part, for they were careful not to address each other directly unless it was unavoidable and then with a politeness which was quite awe-inspiring. But neither gentleman gave any hint of unease; they talked at random about the contents of the newspapers, the forthcoming marriage of Jorina and the possibility of skating if the frost held for a few days more. This remark prompted Julia to ask if everyone skated as a matter of course.

'Certainly we do,' said Ivo. 'We learn as soon as we can toddle and we skate every winter until our legs grow too stiff to support us. Do you skate, Julia?'

'A little—not very well. I fall down a lot.'

'How fortunate,' said Marcia sweetly, 'that there's plenty of you to take the shock.' She laughed as she said it so that everyone should know that it was a joke, and Julia, not to be outdone, laughed too.

'Falling down doesn't matter in the least,' said Ivo, just as though Marcia hadn't spoken. 'We all do it at first. A little practice and you'll be as good as everyone else.'

The conversation took on a new lease of life; they

talked about sport in its various forms for the rest of
the meal. But the meal couldn't last for ever; presently Julia found herself in the sitting room with Doctor van den Werff, listening to the receding footsteps
of Marcia and Ivo crossing the hall to his study.

They came back almost an hour later, Marcia looking very pleased with herself and Ivo looking bland.
Only when Julia looked at him closely she saw that
his eyes weren't bland at all. She sat stubbornly in
her chair, looking serenely unaware of anything un-
toward. If she was to be hauled over the coals then
and now, he could get on with it. She told herself she
hadn't any intention of running away, nor was she
afraid of him. All the same, when after half an hour
of desultory talk, first Marcia and then Doctor van
den Werff got up to go to bed, she felt decidedly
nervous, but she sat on. She had bought some wool
before Christmas to knit herself a sweater; she plied
her needles now as though her very life depended on
getting it finished within the next hour or so.

Ivo spoke and she dropped a stitch. 'You know
what Marcia wanted to see me about?'

She skewered the stitch. 'Yes—at least I think I
do.'

'Did you call her a fraud, Julia?'

Her needles click-clacked along half a row. 'Yes.'

'May I ask why?'

'No harm in asking,' said Julia flippantly, and fell
to counting stitches.

'You also called her a harpy?'

'Thirty-six, thirty-seven...' she raised her head.
'Quite right.' After a moment she asked, 'Did I say
thirty-seven?'

He said nastily, 'Put that damn knitting down—you're only using it to hide behind.'

Julia flared up at this undoubtedly true remark. 'I am not! I could have sneaked off to bed...'

'And I,' he said silkily, 'would have come and hauled you out again.' He got up and walked to the window and back again. 'Why did you do it, Julia? Why in heaven's name...' He came to a halt in front of her chair and stood looking down at her. His voice was calm now even though she was aware that he was seething with rage. 'Couldn't you have left well alone?'

She wondered what he meant by that. She began, 'Do you know—'and stopped. Impossible to tell him about August de Winter being there that afternoon; for a moment she wondered if that was what Marcia had told him too, in which case he already knew. But he didn't, for he said in a reasonable voice—the kind of voice an exasperated grown-up might have used to an annoying child—'Marcia had been alone all day; probably she had become lonely and low-spirited, and you burst in without any warning and call her a—a harpy!' A muscle at the side of his mouth twitched as he said it.

Julia gathered up her knitting. 'Is that what she told you?' she asked. 'Then why bother to ask me? I'm so obviously in the wrong, aren't I?'

She got to her feet and swept out of the room, her lovely head high. In her room she undressed rapidly and when she was ready for bed, sat down and laboriously unpicked the knitting she had done, for the pattern was sadly awry, crying silently as she did so.

She was greeted at breakfast by Doctor van den

Werff's friendly good morning and by Ivo's bland pleasantness. Both gentlemen, after taking a searching glance at her face, refrained from hoping that she had had a good night, desired her to help herself to anything she required, and went back to the discussion they had been having when she joined them.

'I shall go to Sneek,' said Doctor van den Werff. 'Your grandfather's house is there and empty most of the year. I shall enjoy living in it and I can indulge in a little gentle sailing when I feel like it. And of course you can all come for holidays whenever you wish; think how convenient it will be to send the children up to me later on.' He added a little wistfully, 'Your mother was very happy there.'

Ivo said, 'Yes,' in a quiet voice and then more briskly, 'A little young to retire, isn't it, Vader?' He smiled across the table. 'Barely sixty.'

'Oh, I daresay I'll do a little part-time work of some sort, but I shall enjoy my freedom. You'll need a partner, Ivo. Theo, if he'll consider it in a year or so.'

'Yes, of course, but there's time enough…a year, two. You're not in too great a hurry, I hope, Vader?'

'No, and there's a good deal to be done to the house in Sneek—' He went on to enumerate such alterations as he had in mind and Julia stared at her empty plate, half listening. So Ivo had made a decision to marry Marcia; yesterday evening probably when they had been so long in his study and Marcia had looked so pleased with herself—as well she might with the prospect of living in the lovely old house for the rest of her days and with Ivo for a husband. She finished her coffee and when the doctor paused she said in a quiet little voice,

'I should like to return to England as soon as it can be arranged, doctor. I—I've been offered a job in my old hospital. They don't want to wait and I'm not needed here any more; I'm only wasting your money.'

If Doctor van den Werff was surprised at her request, shot at him out of the blue in such a fashion, he said nothing about it, merely looked at her with sharp blue eyes and said, 'Ah, yes, of course, Julia. We shall finish at the school today, so supposing we have a little talk—let me see—tomorrow morning. That gives us plenty of time.'

She agreed, wondering why they should need time; he must have known that it was time for her to leave them. She went to get her coat and came d nstairs in time to hear Ivo say, 'I'll deal with it in my own way…' He stopped when he saw her and she was left to speculate as to exactly what he was intending to deal with. She sat in the car beside him, cudgelling her brains, and came to no conclusion at all. They were almost in Oisterwijk when he asked, 'This job— have you been offered it, Julia?'

She was, on the whole, a truthful girl, so she said now, 'Well, not exactly—but they said when I left they would always have me back.'

'So you have arranged nothing? You have no job to go to?'

She said crossly, because he had found her out in her small deception.

'Please don't bother about me. I shall go to my brother's in any case for a short time.'

'Ah, yes,' she heard the faint mockery in his voice, 'and from what you have told me, you will enjoy that.'

They had arrived at the schoolhouse. She made a small frustrated sound and got out of the car and went inside to where the last remnant of their patients awaited them.

CHAPTER NINE

THEY WERE finished before midday. The last patient went through the door and the clearing up began at once and was quickly done now that there was a sufficiency of nurses and helpers. Ivo had a brief conversation in Dutch with his father and then said to Julia,

'You'll go home with Father, please, I shan't be coming home just yet,' and then to his father, this time in English, 'You'll do those visits for me? I'll fit in the rest when I come back.'

He lifted a hand to them both and went away and a little later Julia got into Doctor van den Werff's car and went back to the house. But when they arrived he made no effort to get out with her, remarking mildly,

'No, I'm not coming in—I've a couple of visits, I'll do them now. Don't wait lunch—I'll get some coffee and something to eat.'

He reversed the car and shot back down the lane. He drove with the same speed and skill as his son, and Julia, watching him go, felt a little pang, because she liked him very much. It was a pity that his wife had died ten years ago; Jorina had told her that her parents had been devoted to each other and that they had been—still were—a close-knit family. Julia went into the house, thinking that at least he would never be lonely with his grandchildren of the future visiting him at Sneek. He would be a delightful grandfather, just as Ivo would be a delightful father to his children, which, thought Julia sourly, would be a good thing if they were to have Marcia for a mother.

She found Marcia already in the dining room and with a brief hullo she sat down opposite her and helped herself to coffee, and because she didn't want Marcia to know how worried she was, she ate a good lunch, choking down every mouthful with a determination which did her credit, while Marcia, in a silence which could be felt, watched her. They separated after the meal, Marcia to return to the sitting room and Julia to go to her room where she wrote a letter to her brother, a letter which took some time and much thought before she was satisfied with it. It was almost four o'clock by the time she was ready and she went downstairs again; there would be tea presently in the sitting room. She went in and was at once aware that a storm was about to break over her head.

Marcia was sitting by the fire, not in her usual graceful semi-recumbent position, but upright, ready to do battle, her fingers beating a tattoo on the book she was holding. Julia watched the fingers, thankful to know that Marcia was as nervous as she was, and decided not to sit down. She felt, quite erroneously, that while she was on her feet she had a slight advantage. She wandered over to the old gilded mirror hanging beside the fireplace and composedly straightened her cap, waiting for her companion to speak. She didn't have to wait very long; Marcia flung her book from her and said in a high voice,

'I suppose you think I can't see through your little

gamc, Nurse Pennyfeather. Ivo would be a fine catch for a penniless half-educated girl such as you are, wouldn't he? You could lead a lady's life, no doubt. I wonder what you did in order to persuade him to bring you here in the first place—and ruby earrings indeed! I wonder what you did to get those?'

She paused, staring at Julia with spiteful eyes, and Julia, her teeth clenched to guard a fierce impulsive tongue, carefully tucked a stray end under her cap and miraculously said nothing.

'You've forced yourself upon him; do you think I haven't seen you laughing at him and talking silly nonsense to make him laugh too—getting lost in order to attract attention to yourself; pretending that you're interested in learning Dutch? Well, it's done you no good, has it? I talked to Ivo, you see—Oh, I didn't tell tales, I'm not such a fool,' she laughed, 'but I suggested this and hinted at that and let a few things drop…he thinks nothing of you now; once you're back in England he'll forget you, and you can go when you like—you're no longer my nurse.'

'As to that,' said Julia calmly, 'I don't feel I can do that. Doctor van den Werff is my employer, you know. I'll go when he tells me to. You could of course ask him to dismiss me, but you would have to give some reason for that. You tried once before without much success, didn't you?' She took out her compact and powdered her beautiful nose, and the action calmed her so that she was able to ask without heat,

'Why do you want Ivo to think you're in love with him? It would be easy enough to tell him that you wanted to marry Mijnheer de Winter, wouldn't it?'

Marcia smiled. 'You're a fool, aren't you? I shall

go on letting Ivo think that I'm in love with him until you've gone back to England, then I can drop him when I'm ready, once August...' She paused and asked with genuine astonishment, 'You don't think I'll step down for you, do you?'

Julia turned back to the mirror and started, quite unnecessarily, on her hair once more because it would keep her calm and she needed all the calm she could muster. She was about to speak when she saw that the half-open door reflected in the mirror had been opened wider and Ivo was standing there. She had no idea how long he had been there or how much he had heard. She drew a deep breath to stop the pounding of her heart and raised her voice, speaking in loud clear tones, calculated to reach his ears.

'No,' she said, 'I didn't, but I'm not quite a fool, you know. You never needed a nurse; I imagine that you were walking quite well some time before I came. I wondered about that a lot, but it wasn't until yesterday afternoon when I saw you and Mijnheer de Winter kissing each other that I knew for certain. You've been using Ivo for your own ends, haven't you, because you don't love him, do you? You have no idea what loving someone is, although you and Mijnheer de Winter enjoy a desiccated form of it, I suppose—quoting Latin tags.' She turned away from the mirror and looked at Marcia. 'How dare you,' she was speaking, if anything, louder than ever in her anxiety that Ivo shouldn't miss a word, 'use Ivo to egg on that miserable little man—Ivo's worth a hundred of him!' She saw, out of the corner of her eye, that Ivo had moved. 'I said you were a fraud and a harpy, and I'll say it again...'

She was interrupted by Ivo's voice, so cold that it sent a shiver down her spine. 'That will do, Julia, and you had no reason to raise your voice like that, you know, I heard you very easily. Perhaps you would be good enough to leave us. I think Marcia and I have—er—a misunderstanding to clear up.'

He was standing in front of her now and when she looked at him and met his eyes, it was to find them hooded like his father's and the calmness of his face told her nothing. She turned on her heel and left them together.

It took her just under ten minutes to change out of her uniform and into her outdoor clothes, and in that time, too, she packed her case. It took her another two minutes to write a very brief note to Doctor van der Werff and count the money in her purse. She had ample to get her back to England and once she was there she didn't much mind what happened. She closed her door soundlessly, then went quietly down the stairs and out of the front door and down the lane to the road. Her case was heavy, but she didn't notice that; she was busy trying to remember about buses and trains and boats to England; she would go to Oisterwijk first, because she could catch a bus to Tilburg from there, and in Tilburg she could get on a train to Rotterdam and go on to the Hook of Holland in time to pick up the night boat. She had plenty of time, even allowing for the walk to Oisterwijk, and she thought it unlikely that anyone would notice her absence for an hour or two and by then she would be in the train, and Ivo and Marcia would have had their talk and cleared up their misunderstandings and either become reconciled—with a suitable Latin tag, she thought wildly, or agreed to part, in either case they would be far too concerned with their own affairs to worry about her.

She shivered in the cold wind and looked doubtfully at the sky, along whose horizon great sulky clouds were piling themselves; it only needed to snow. She walked on steadily, her mind quite empty of thought now, although now and again she looked behind her at the singularly empty road, because hope dies hard and although she tried to damp down the thought, Ivo might come after her. She had thought once or twice hat he might love her a little, but now she didn't know any more. If he did he would surely follow her; she took one final look down the empty road. Apparently he wasn't going to; she must be out of her mind to even entertain the idea.

She reached the bus stop at last and joined the queue, which wasn't a queue at all but just a large group of people who, when the bus arrived, would jostle and push their way on to it in a good-natured and ruthless manner; she would have to be ruthless too; it would never do to he left behind. She put down her case and looked about her. Her companions were mostly women with shopping baskets and children, although there were one or two men, standing rock firm, well to the front. She hoped the bus would be along soon and wouldn't be too full as she looked nervously at the sky. As she did so a snowflake fell softly on to her nose.

The Jensen snarled to a halt beside her and Ivo got out, put her case on the back seat and said in a voice which gave nothing away,

'Get in, Julia.' She didn't budge, and the women

on either side of her turned to look, arranging their baskets comfortably over their arms; it was dull waiting for the bus and here was a small diversion—besides, they knew Ivo by sight. He smiled at them and raised his hat and murmured, '*Dag, Dames,*' and they chorused a '*Dag, Doctor,*' back at him, pleased to be recognised. He said something else to them too, to make them smile and nudge each other and stare with curious friendly eyes at Julia.

'Don't be pig-headed, dear girl,' he said in English, 'they're on my side.' He laughed a little and she found her voice at last, treacherously shaky.

'I couldn't care less,' she said pettishly, and then, because she couldn't help herself, 'How did you know I'd be here?'

'A process of elimination.' His voice was very decided as he went on, 'Now get in, my dear, because the car's on a bus stop and I'm in grave danger of getting a *procesverbaal.*'

She didn't know what that was, but it sounded official and she concluded that it was, for as the car slid away from the pavement a policeman on a bicycle came towards them in a purposeful way. Ivo waved to him and the man looked at him and smiled and cycled on. Ivo turned the car and sped back the way she had come, all without saying a word. It was only when, to her bewilderment, they had passed the house and he had turned the Jensen into a country road leading out into the heath that he slowed his pace and asked gently,

'Dear heart, why did you go, without a word to anyone and in such a hurry?' and when she made a small sound of protest: 'Oh, I've got your note to Father in my pocket. Tell me.'

She savoured the delight of being his dear heart and then said in a low voice, 'I couldn't have stayed. You see, it was deliberate—all the things I said to Marcia; I saw you in the mirror and I wanted you to hear, and then I—I thought how awful if you loved her after all and I'd spoilt it all for you for always, so I went away quickly because it wouldn't have taken you long to discover—Marcia would have…'

Julia stopped speaking because she felt like crying and she would have to conquer her desire to burst into tears before she could continue.

'I had no idea that you were such a virago,' remarked Ivo on a half laugh, 'but I did tell you to leave well alone, Julia, my darling. Do you think that I am blind—though I have been blind, haven't I? But I had to talk to de Winter and make sure that I was justified in breaking the imaginary understanding I was supposed to have with Marcia.'

Julia heaved a gulping sob. 'Oh, dear,' she sounded forlorn, 'I needn't have said any of those awful things, but I didn't know…' She looked out of the car window and said uncertainly, 'I got lost here…'

Ivo had halted the car. He got out and went round the bonnet, helped her out and took her arm and started walking over the bone-hard ground towards the woods.

'So did I, my dear darling, at least my heart did—to you.' He stopped and turned her round to face him, then bent his head and kissed her mouth. 'That's not quite true,' he said a long minute later, 'I lost it when you opened the door at Drumlochie House and told me in your lovely voice to hurry up and come in out of the cold. My Julia, I've not been cold since because you warm me with your sweetness and gaiety and beauty. But it was here I found you curled up asleep and I knew when I saw you that I couldn't go on without you. I've brought you here to tell you so.'

They had reached the edge of the trees by now and he stopped again, but Julia held back a little. 'Marcia,' she demanded, 'did she mind?'

Ivo shook his head. 'I don't imagine so—you see, de Winter said that he would come and fetch her within the hour and she and I—we had known that we had no feeling for each other, and you know why I couldn't break with her, not until I knew for certain about de Winter. She'll marry him and live happily ever after.'

'Reading Greek poetry to each other,' said Julia, and added in a doubtful voice, 'I'm not a clever girl,' and was gathered close and kissed by way of a very satisfactory answer.

'My darling girl, I want a wife, not a walking dictionary. A wife who is so beautiful that I can't stop looking at her or thinking about her and who buys extravagant clothes and wants diamonds for her birthday and makes bread and loves children—and loves me.'

'I like the bit about the diamonds,' said Julia. 'It's very tempting, but I can't say yes if you don't ask me.'

She stared up at him, her face glowing and her eyes bright and Ivo said, 'I should have asked you the moment I set eyes on you. Will you marry me, my darling Julia?'

Julia smiled. 'Yes, thank you, Ivo, I will. Indeed I don't know what else I would have done if you didn't want me.'

There was only one answer to a remark like that. When at length Ivo loosed her, he asked, 'Do you know which day it is, my dearest?'

Julia, deep in her own delightful thoughts, frowned. 'December the twenty-ninth,' she said at length.

'The fifth day of Christmas,' said Ivo. 'You said once that five gold rings would be more than any girl could want and I said it was a way in which her true love could prove to her that he loved her.'

He took an arm from her shoulders and plunged a hand into his pocket, then opened his hand to show her what he held.

'You see? I went to the Hague and got them after I had seen de Winter. I couldn't think of a better way of convincing you that I love you and always shall.'

He looked at her very tenderly as he pushed the fur bonnet back so that he could hook the little gold rings in her ears. 'I cheated a little with this one,' he said as he fastened the gold bracelet on one wrist, 'but not with this.' He pulled off her glove and slipped a gold ring, set with three most beautiful diamonds, on to her finger. 'And this one—you'll have to wait for this one, my dearest, until we marry.'

Julia watched the diamonds sparkle in the deepening dusk and then stretched up to kiss him. 'Thank you five times, darling Ivo, and when will that be?'

His arm tightened around her so that she could scarcely breathe.

He said, 'We'll wait until the polio scare is over, then we'll go to England and I'll get a special licence.

Unless you want a grand wedding with a cake and
bridesmaids?' He kissed her gently and then with
great fierceness. 'In which case we should have to
wait. Please don't make me wait, Julia.'

She closed her eyes with resolution upon a tanta-
lizing vision of herself in white satin and a tulle veil.
She said clearly, 'I don't want to wait either, Ivo.'
She paused to smile at him. 'We'll find a small church
in the country and just get married.'

She was going to enlarge upon this idea, but was
prevented from doing so because Ivo kissed her again,
a long, gentle, satisfying kiss. When she had her
breath again she added, 'I shall, of course, wear my
five gold rings!'

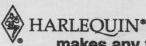

HARLEQUIN®
makes any time special—online...

eHARLEQUIN.com

shop eHarlequin

- ❦ Find all the new Harlequin releases at everyday great discounts.
- ❦ Try before you buy! Read an excerpt from the latest Harlequin novels.
- ❦ Write an online review and share your thoughts with others.

reading room

- ❦ Read our Internet exclusive daily and weekly online serials, or vote in our interactive novel.
- ❦ Talk to other readers about your favorite novels in our Reading Groups.
- ❦ Take our Choose-a-Book quiz to find the series that matches you!

authors' alcove

- ❦ Find out interesting tidbits and details about your favorite authors' lives, interests and writing habits.
- ❦ Ever dreamed of being an author? Enter our Writing Round Robin. The Winning Chapter will be published online! Or review our writing guidelines for submitting your novel.

All this and more available at
www.eHarlequin.com
on Women.com Networks

REGENCY
ROMANCE

Transport yourself to the grace and charm
of an era gone by...where opulence is the
rule and captivating adventures between
feisty heroines and roguish heroes
entertain with enchanting wit.

*Experience the enchanting world of Regency romance
in November 2001 with these four titles:*

THE SILVER SQUIRE
by Mary Brendan

A BARGAIN WITH FATE
by Ann Elizabeth Cree

LADY KNIGHTLEY'S
SECRET
by Anne Ashley

THE ADMIRAL'S
DAUGHTER
by Francesca Shaw

If you enjoyed what you just read,
then we've got an offer you can't resist!

Take 2
bestselling novels FREE!
Plus get a FREE surprise gift!

Clip this page and mail it to The Best of the Best™

IN U.S.A.
3010 Walden Ave.
P.O. Box 1867
Buffalo, N.Y. 14240-1867

IN CANADA
P.O. Box 609
Fort Erie, Ontario
L2A 5X3

YES! Please send me 2 free Best of the Best™ novels and my free surprise gift. After receiving them, if I don't wish to receive anymore, I can return the shipping statement marked cancel. If I don't cancel, I will receive 4 brand-new novels every month, before they're available in stores! In the U.S.A., bill me at the bargain price of $4.24 plus 25¢ shipping and handling per book and applicable sales tax, if any*. In Canada, bill me at the bargain price of $4.74 plus 25¢ shipping and handling per book and applicable taxes**. That's the complete price and a savings of over 15% off the cover prices—what a great deal! I understand that accepting the 2 free books and gift places me under no obligation ever to buy any books. I can always return a shipment and cancel at any time. Even if I never buy another book from The Best of the Best™, the 2 free books and gift are mine to keep forever.

185 MEN DFNG
385 MEN DFNH

Name	(PLEASE PRINT)	
Address	Apt.#	
City	State/Prov.	Zip/Postal Code

* Terms and prices subject to change without notice. Sales tax applicable in N.Y.
** Canadian residents will be charged applicable provincial taxes and GST.
  All orders subject to approval. Offer limited to one per household and not valid to current Best of the Best™ subscribers.
  ® are registered trademarks of Harlequin Enterprises Limited.

BOB01 ©1998 Harlequin Enterprises Limited